"We don't have to go to [...] whispered.

"So if you're doing this out of a sense of duty, you don't need to."

Nick smiled as he unfastened a button. "Talia, I promise you, there is absolutely not one tiny shred of feeling that I have a duty to perform here." She could hear the amusement in his voice. He unfastened another button, pushed the dress open. "This isn't a chore for me," he said as his smile faded and his voice became hoarse, breathless.

"You'll complicate our lives from the first night we're together," she warned.

"I might do that," he said, his hungry gaze making her heart pound. "We complicated it when we married, and we knew we had complicated it after that first kiss."

They were married, man and wife, and she wanted it all with him, and at the moment she was reckless and eager enough to risk her heart.

"Nick, I want you, but I'm warning you, my body comes with a heart inside and emotions all tangled with sex. You're taking a risk here just as much as I am."

"After hearing your first words before your warning, I'm willing to take the risk," he whispered gruffly as he showered kisses on her throat and down her neck.

* * *

Married for His Heir is part of Harlequin Desire's #1 bestselling series, Billionaires and Babies: Powerful men...wrapped around their babies' little fingers.

Dear Reader,

Married for His Heir is about the risks in life and love, when the heart is involved. Even a handsome Texas rancher's billions cannot protect him from suffering when his wife and baby son are killed. Nick Duncan has been hurt so badly by his losses, he doesn't want to open his heart again and be torn apart the way he was in the past.

Also with a painful past, after trying to guard her heart, Talia Barton realizes living life fully includes taking chances on getting hurt.

Into her life and Nick's comes a precious baby girl who needs their love. Knowing she will be heartbroken, Talia pours out her love for the orphaned toddler, as well as for Nick. At the same time, determined to avoid more heartrending losses, Nick closes his aching heart. It's another Texas story where a baby girl changes lives, and as babies do, brings the miracle of love to everyone around her.

Thank you for your interest in this book. Find me on Facebook as Sara Orwig, Romance Writer or go to my website, saraorwig.com.

Best wishes,

Sara Orwig

SARA ORWIG

MARRIED FOR HIS HEIR

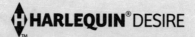

Recycling programs
for this product may
not exist in your area.

ISBN-13: 978-1-335-97135-7

Married for His Heir

Copyright © 2018 by Sara Orwig

Printed in U.S.A.

Sara Orwig, from Oklahoma, loves family, friends, dogs, books, long walks, sunny beaches and palm trees. She is married to and in love with the guy she met in college. They have three children and six grandchildren. Sara's 100th published novel was a July 2016 release. With a master's degree in English, Sara has written historical romance, mainstream fiction and contemporary romance. Sara welcomes readers on Facebook or at saraorwig.com.

Books by Sara Orwig

Harlequin Desire

Callahan's Clan

Expecting the Rancher's Child
The Rancher's Baby Bargain
The Rancher's Cinderella Bride
The Texan's Baby Proposal

Texas Promises

Expecting a Lone Star Heir

Billionaires and Babies

Married for His Heir

Visit her Author Profile page at Harlequin.com, or saraorwig.com, for more titles.

With thanks to Stacy Boyd,
who made this book possible.

Thank you to Tahra Seplowin for fixing things
and answering questions.

With thanks always to Maureen Walters.

Also, with love to my family,
who fill my days with joy.

One

"Just remember, curiosity killed the cat." Nick Duncan shot his brother a narrow-eyed look, as if willing him to lay off.

But Stan didn't take the hint. He merely shook his head and continued. "What do you expect, Nick? A woman you don't know is coming by to tell you about an inheritance you didn't know you had. Of course I'm curious."

Nick had to agree, the man had a point.

He stepped off the porch into the front yard of his cattle ranch, the ND Ranch, taking a moment to let his gaze sweep over the landscaped front yard, green from the constant watering. But nothing could distract his thoughts. An inheritance?

"And you say our attorney told you to accept the appointment with her?" Stan asked, stepping up beside his oldest brother.

"Yeah. Apparently, she went to Horace and talked to him instead of calling me. How she found him, I don't know. That should be personal information." He swiped a hand across his neck. "I've been racking my brain, but heck, I don't know any Talia Barton, not in the oil business, not from ranching, not socially. And I'm sure I'd remember. Since I stepped down as CEO at Duncan Energy, I don't stay in Dallas. Only when I have to go to board meetings or something special. This ranch is where I live. I can't think of any woman named Talia. There have been so damn few women in my life since I became a widower."

"You mean no one that you've been interested in," Stan clarified. "You have a steady stream of women coming to see you, bringing you enough casseroles and desserts to open a restaurant out here. I'll bet you have a fridge filled with food in your Dallas house, too."

"Oh, yeah. The ladies don't want me to starve. They've got good intentions, but I'm not interested." He hadn't been interested in a woman in three years—and he didn't figure he ever would be again.

He took off his Stetson and swiped it across his jean-clad thigh, as if he could banish the memories as easily as he did the dust on his hat. All this time and thoughts of Regina could creep up on him at the oddest times.

He squared his shoulders and replaced the hat. "Well, no matter who she is, this Talia Barton can come out here to see me. I'm not driving to Dallas. I told Horace."

He'd also asked the attorney questions. Lots of them. But he hadn't gotten any answers. Whatever this mystery woman had told Horace, he wouldn't say. He'd merely insisted Nick make an appointment to meet her.

"Is Horace coming to the ranch?"

"No, I told him he didn't need to. Whatever she intends to do, this meeting should be short." Nick turned to his brother, looking into eyes that were as green as his own, and flecked with gold. "Come to think of it, Stan, you might as well stay. Whatever inheritance I'm getting, it may eventually involve you."

"Oh, no," Stan said, grinning. "I have my new horse loaded into my trailer and I'm taking him home. I'll hear later what the mysterious Ms. Barton is giving you. And, by the way, have you told Grandmother?"

Nick rolled his eyes. "Are you kidding? Of course not. At least not until I know why we're meeting."

Stan laughed. "No, I guess not. I sure as hell wouldn't tell her until I knew and maybe not even then."

Nick clapped his brother on the back. "Come

on—let's go inside. I'm not waiting out here to greet Ms. Barton," he said, turning for his ranch home.

"No, no." Stan shook his head. "I told you, I'm leaving. This appointment is for you and it's private. You can call and tell me what the hell a woman you don't even know has for you."

"I'm still tempted to ignore Horace and refuse to see her."

"Horace has been our family attorney for years and your attorney since you turned twenty-one. You do what he says and meet with her. You know he's not giving you bad advice."

"I don't know. Any attorney who won't confide in his own client whom he has known since I was five years old is a damn poor attorney, if you ask me."

"You know Horace has to have a good reason for not telling you what's involved." Stan started to leave, his wavy brown hair tangling in the breeze. "And it must be something good."

"If it isn't, I'm getting a new attorney," Nick grumbled, gazing down the long ranch drive that disappeared around a curve where a tall cottonwood's leaves fluttered in the wind.

Stan left, his boots clicking on the brick walk as he headed to his shiny black pickup with a horse trailer hitched to it.

While he rubbed the brown stubble covering his jaw, Nick watched the plume of gray dust Stan's truck stirred as he drove away. In minutes the dust settled and he went inside to wait in the study. He only wished his thoughts could settle just as easily. But he couldn't still the questions that swirled in his mind.

Talia Barton…

Since he had become a widower, he'd had a few one-nighters, all meaningless encounters, but not many of them and not in a long time. He had been working late hours to wear himself out, and working out before and after handling ranch tasks. He didn't date and he didn't want to. So how did he know Talia Barton?

It was fifteen anguishing minutes later when he heard a car pull up the ranch drive. He went to the window and watched as a black car slowed and stopped in front of the house.

In minutes the driver emerged from the car and Nick's interest increased a fraction as he viewed a tall, leggy blonde in high heels, a navy suit and a white blouse. Looking as if she had just stepped out of an office or a photo shoot, she would turn heads wherever she went. If she had any persuasive abilities, he could see why Horace had told him to meet her.

He forced himself to stand still. His house manager served as a butler, and since Royce knew she was coming, he would bring her to the study. Instead, Nick watched her come up the steps and his pulse jumped. The woman was gorgeous.

He walked across the room to the open door. In seconds he heard Royce talking to her, and when they came into sight, Nick stepped forward. "Thanks, Royce." He extended his hand to the woman. "Ms. Barton, I'm Nick Duncan," he said as Royce left them.

The moment he wrapped his hand around her soft, warm hand, he felt a sizzling jolt of awareness, something that hadn't happened since his wife. The reaction startled him and he looked more closely at her.

He saw a flicker in her thickly lashed blue eyes that caused his pulse to jump another notch. She felt something, too, and that knowledge fueled his reaction.

She cleared her throat and withdrew her hand. "I'm Talia Barton. Please call me Talia," she said in a soft voice. There was a directness about her that made him feel she was a no-nonsense person, and once again, he thought that people probably did what she wanted.

"Come have a seat where we can talk," he urged, motioning her into the study. "I'm curious what it is that you couldn't tell me about by phone," he said, his interest growing because he was absolutely certain he had never seen this woman in his life before now. He would not forget her. "My attorney has urged me to see you, so whatever it is, you've certainly convinced him."

"I think you'll agree after you hear me out," she said, following him into the room. She took the leather chair he indicated and sat facing him.

Nick couldn't resist looking when she crossed her long, shapely legs. His reaction to her startled him again. He hadn't had this kind of response to a woman since his wife's death almost three years ago. The anniversary of the plane crash that had taken his wife and baby would be in August. Since his loss, it was as if he had become numb, half dead himself and oblivious of women, except for a few one-nighters at parties far from the ranch.

Why was he having this reaction to this mystery woman?

Talia looked into green eyes flecked with gold and realized there would be nothing easy about this meeting. To add to her jittery nerves, Nick Duncan was not only handsome and appealing, but there was some kind of vibrant chemistry between them.

In every way she possibly could, including hiring a private investigator to get information on Nick, Talia had checked into his life. To her relief, all sources reported that Nick Duncan was intelligent, reliable, capable, confident, successful and tough when he needed to be. From all that she could find out, he had been a good husband and father, even though he'd had his son for only a brief time.

Once he'd checked out, she'd gone ahead with her plans to meet him and lay out her problem for him. But she hadn't planned on this volatile chemistry that had simmered between them from the moment she had walked into the room.

When they had shaken hands the sizzle had startled her. So had the tingles when she'd met his gaze. It wouldn't matter, though, she told herself, because they would never mean anything to each other. Still, she had been surprised. Since her disastrous marriage while still in college and then divorce, she hadn't been drawn to any man. Besides, there was too much upheaval in her life now. But somehow, with a mere touch, Nick Duncan broke through all that. He was far more handsome and sexy in person than his pictures indicated. It wasn't even his personality because he was being polite, cautious and reserved. She knew he wondered why she was there and what she wanted. She might as well tell him and get this over with.

Nothing in her life—not the deaths in her family or her broken marriage—had hurt as much as this. Tears threatened, uncustomary for her, and she swallowed, looking around the room as she fought to get her emotions under control. She had rehearsed what she would say to him, but now that the moment had come and she was actually facing him, she wanted to run to her car and drive home.

And then what? she asked herself. If she didn't talk to him, the alternative was worse. Nick Duncan had checked out as a successful, intelligent, family-oriented man. A billionaire, owner of the ND Ranch, part owner of Duncan Energy, a company started by his father and now run by the two youngest Duncan brothers with Nick and his brother Stan on the

board. Nick was a good rancher, a good business-
man, a man who had had his own terrible loss. She
had no choice but to do what she'd come here to
do. She squared her shoulders and sat up straight,
but before she could speak, he broke the awkward
silence.

"Do you live around here?" he asked.

"I live in Dallas. I teach art in a two-year college."

He didn't know it, but his question gave her the
opening she needed. She took a breath and gave
him a faint smile.

"Mr. Duncan, I'm—"

"Nick, please," he prompted her.

"Yes, well, Nick, I'm sure you're curious as to
why I wanted to see you…and there's no need to
wait. I want your help about something belonging
to you."

He leaned in closer, resting his hands on his
knees as he looked at her intently.

"I've had a neighbor whose niece, Madeline Prentiss, inherited her house and Madeline and I became
friends. Neither of us have any family, so we were
drawn together. She had a degree and internship
in landscape architecture. She worked for a landscape company and took a night art class I taught
because she drew landscape plans for clients. We
rode to class together that year and became even
closer friends."

She related the facts, the history that he needed to

know, but the whole time she spoke, all she wanted to do was leave. She didn't want to ask his help or ask him to do anything. She took a deep breath, looking into those curious green-gold eyes that made her heart beat faster, and suddenly she couldn't go on. They stared at each other.

"I had this all rehearsed," she said finally as she rose abruptly, "but it isn't easy. Just give me a minute."

"Sure. Take your time. Let me get you a glass of water," he said, getting up and leaving the room. She suspected he did it to give her a moment to get herself composed. She knew what she had to do. When he returned, he held a tray with a pitcher and two glasses of ice and water. He handed her one, and when their fingers brushed, for just an instant, she felt another flash of intense awareness of him as an appealing man. While she sipped the icy water, her gaze locked with his. The look in his eyes made her heartbeat quicken.

"Want to have a seat?" he said, setting the tray on a table. As they sat down again, she noticed his gaze on her as she crossed her legs. She placed her glass on a coaster on a small table beside her chair and adjusted her skirt.

"This is hard for me, Mr. Dunc—er, Nick—but it is definitely overdue. I was telling you about a friend of mine, Madeline Prentiss."

He nodded. "Is there a reason you're telling me all this about this particular person?"

"Yes. I'm here because of Madeline. You see, almost two years ago when Madeline was at a party in Austin, she had a romantic night with a man she met there but she never saw him again."

"I take it Madeline thinks I'm that man?"

"Yes. You were that man. That's definite, and in the past, she told me about the night you two had." She leaned in and had no choice but to gather her courage and blurt it out. "And there's a baby from that encounter."

Stunned, Nick felt as if ice water had been poured over him.

"You're saying that I fathered a baby with this woman? And I've never heard a word from her about it? Why did she wait until now and why send you? Where is Madeline now?" He couldn't stop the questions that spilled from his lips. Though part of him was in shock, the other part was in overdrive, and he wanted—no, needed—answers.

"Madeline didn't want to inform you of her pregnancy because that night, you spent a long time telling her how much you loved your wife. You told her about losing your little two-month-old son and your wife in a plane crash. You also convinced her that you missed your wife and you weren't ready to go out with anyone else. She told me you actually cried over your loss. Besides, she knew that you weren't in love with her and probably never would be."

"You're using the past tense." A chill skittered up his spine.

"That's right," Talia acknowledged. But she didn't elaborate. Instead she said, "Madeline had a talent. She could sing and she had gotten auditions and began to get bookings that paid more than the landscape business."

He suddenly remembered Madeline, because she had sung at the party the night he met her. Talia was right: she had talent.

"You remember her," Talia said, startling him that she guessed his thoughts so easily.

"It's a little blurry, but I do. I don't go out much, so there aren't many occasions to even try to recall, but I remember her because she was beautiful and talented. She sang for everyone that night."

"Madeline was on the way to a successful singing career, until several months ago when she was killed in a car wreck. She was young and she didn't leave a will. Since her death I've been caring for her baby, and now I'm in a fight with the state, which wants to take her precious baby away. I've pulled every string I can, but I'm not a relative nor the legal guardian of Madeline's baby. Madeline left no directive, nothing to indicate that she would want to appoint me guardian of her baby. She had no family, either. You, on the other hand, are her baby's blood father."

He barely heard what she went on to say to him.

His mind was stuck on one phrase. ...*baby's blood father...*

He was the father of a baby.

A baby he didn't know with a deceased mother he barely remembered.

"Sorry, give me a second. This is a shock." He reached for his water and took a gulp. What he really needed was something far stronger. "When you said you needed to see me, I didn't dream it would be about a baby. My baby. A baby that's an orphan."

"Not really an orphan," Talia said, looking intently at him. "She has a living blood relative—her father. You. I've checked you out and you have high recommendations as to your character." She paused a second. Then her gaze seemed to deepen as she continued. "I need your help, Nick."

"How's that?" he asked, trying to pay attention and listen to what she was saying, but the shock of learning he had a baby still dominated his attention.

"You can keep the state from taking her."

"Her? A little girl?" he asked, his shock increasing. "I don't know one thing about little girls."

"There was a time you didn't know anything about running a ranch or about baby boys, either."

They stared at each other and he could feel an invisible ripple of conflict. He ignored it.

He had a baby girl whom he'd never seen. That was the only thought that dominated his mind. "How old is she?" he asked her.

"Fourteen months."

"I had a baby boy for two months. He would be two years, nine months old now." Trying to push aside a familiar dull ache at the thought of Regina and Artie, Nick took a deep breath. "Beyond the two months with Artie, I have no experience being a father. It was different when I had a wife and we wanted a family, but... I don't know anything about babies. I don't know anything about little girls..."

His hand practically shook as he put his glass down on the table. The next thought struck him like a raging bull. "You're sure this is my baby?"

Talia showed no reaction. She maintained her composure as she replied. "Yes, Madeline was sure. You can get a DNA test if you'd like. Hattie is her name."

"Hattie's her name?" He liked the way it sounded.

She nodded. "I don't have any doubt about the outcome, but no doubt you'll be reassured when the DNA results prove that Hattie is your little girl."

For a moment they sat in silence as he gazed out the window at his land spreading off in the distance. Was this true? Was he a father again? Even though he had been a father for two months, he couldn't see himself as a dad to a little girl who was over one year old.

He looked back at Talia and met a cool, blue-eyed stare. She impressed him because in her quiet way, even when she didn't want to break the news, she had taken charge of this meeting, something that didn't happen to him with women, except for his grandmother.

"You've been caring for this baby?"

"Yes, I've been keeping Hattie since Madeline's death. I watched Hattie often before Madeline died. As I said, she had no family and I was like a second mama for Hattie. Hattie has been in day care and I pick her up when I leave school. In a few weeks, the spring session will be over and I'm not teaching this summer. I'll take her out of day care and be home with her."

He sat quietly, mulling over all he had learned. How was he going to deal with this? He was a parent who didn't know anything about babies or little girls and he wanted solid proof that this was actually his child.

"I want the DNA test," he said. "Until I have proof, I don't want to do anything."

"I can understand that and I expected you to want confirmation. But you must understand, time is an issue here. However, if I tell the state agents that you're looking into gaining custody of your child, they'll probably back off for a while, especially long enough for you to get a DNA test."

"If they don't, I'll talk to my attorney and we'll deal with them."

She opened her purse, pulled out an envelope and handed it to him. "Here's the name, a number to call and the address for the DNA test. It takes time, but it will prove Hattie is your baby girl. My number is there also."

Nick took the envelope, turning it over in his hand.

"In the meantime," Talia added, "so we don't waste time, I think you should meet Hattie."

Maybe she was right.

He looked up at her. "You sound certain about my parentage. If I get this little child, if she is mine and the state backs off, where do you come in? You've been caring for her."

She shook her head and looked away, and to his shock it looked as if her eyes filled with tears. "I love Hattie like she's my own, but I know I have to give her up. She's your baby. You're young and you'll marry again. I'm realistic enough to know there won't be a place in her life for me once I turn her over to you."

She ran her fingers over her eyes and he knew she wiped away tears. He thought about his own loss. He only knew his son two months, but he had loved him beyond measure, so he could understand her feelings. She'd loved this baby for fourteen months and a lot of that time she had been the sole parent with only the help of the day care. He was sorry that she hurt and he knew the hurt would only grow.

"It's amazing how babies can wrap around your heart and steal it away," he said gently and she gave him a startled glance. "If you live in the area, perhaps we can work something out where you can see her. We'll talk about it after the DNA result is in," he added.

"Thank you. That's nice if it works out," she said, still staring at him as if reassessing her opinion about him. She brushed her fingers over her eyes again and took a deep breath before she spoke. "You're very doubtful this is your baby. I can understand that but—"

"You're certain that Madeline gave you the straight story?" he interrupted to ask her. "I mean, if I am the father, she had almost two years to tell me about the baby."

"I encouraged her to, but in the beginning, she worried that you might try to take Hattie from her. When her music career was beginning to take off she expected to leave Texas and move to New York or California or maybe Nashville, and she figured you'd never cross paths again."

And if that had come to pass, he'd never have known about Hattie. If she was indeed his.

Talia must have read his thoughts because she said, "You get your DNA test and we'll talk." As she stood, he came to his feet immediately. "Unless you have some questions, I think we're finished for now."

"You don't have a doubt, do you?" he asked and looked into her big blue eyes that made him draw a deep breath again and almost forget his question.

"No, I don't. I do want you to know the truth and

the DNA should convince you. That and Hattie's looks."

Startled, he stopped thinking about Talia's blue eyes and stared at her. "You think Hattie looks like me?"

"You can decide when you see her," she said, smiling faintly.

Her smile couldn't hide the hurt that he saw in her eyes. She didn't want to give up the baby she'd come to love. He could see that. He also saw the toll this meeting was taking on her. It was time to end it.

"I'll get the DNA test and we'll get back together," he said as he led her out of the study. "I just can't fully accept this until I have some proof. I'm glad you understand that."

"Yes, I do." She stopped at the front door and turned to him. "You have my name, address and phone number in that envelope. I'll expect to hear from you."

There was authority in her tone that reminded him of his grandmother and he almost felt he should promptly answer, "Yes, ma'am." Instead, as he caught the scent of her perfume and looked into the depths of her eyes, he wanted to ask her out. The idea surprised him, and as fast as it came, he dismissed it. This woman had already complicated his life, and whatever happened, he needed to keep his wits about him and not get emotionally—or physically—involved with her. He wasn't going to consider dealing with Talia if Hattie turned out not to be his baby, either.

Too bad, really. He suspected she was as strong-willed as he was, and under other circumstances he would have liked to get to know her.

Talia reached for the doorknob the instant he did, and instead of the cold metal handle, his hand touched the warm softness of her wrist. Instantly, his heartbeat sped up and he was aware that mere inches separated them. Her skin was smooth and flawless; her rosy mouth was as captivating as her gorgeous blue eyes. When he couldn't get his breath, the reaction she caused in him astonished him. Seconds after he'd lectured himself to resist her appeal, he reacted to it.

His eyes left her lips and traveled to her eyes when her voice broke the silence. "Nick," she said, "I may not have the right to ask you but…" He saw her throat tighten as she swallowed back tears. "If she is your baby and you don't want her, please don't abandon her and let her become a ward of the state. Surely there's room in your life and your heart for a child you've fathered."

"If this is my child, I'll take responsibility," Nick said. He couldn't help wondering if he was making a colossal mistake in committing himself, yet he wouldn't abandon a baby that was his own.

"I'll count on that. You won't regret it. She is an adorable, happy baby," she said, and he heard the wistful note in her voice.

Something hurt deep inside him as he once again thought of his own little boy, who came into his life and then went out too fast. Even though it was approaching three years since he last held Artie, he still hurt badly. "I'll get the DNA and contact you whatever the answer."

She nodded. "I'll be waiting and we can go from there. Thank you for telling me that Hattie can rely on you."

He opened the door and Talia stepped away, but he saw tears in her eyes again. "I'll wait to hear from you."

He watched her walk to her car, her hips swaying slightly with a poised, purposeful walk. She was one good-looking woman, but she had come into his life with potential news that would change it forever. So why the physical reaction to her? Maybe he was coming back to life and would have that reaction with any other attractive woman.

As fast as that thought came, he rejected it. He saw attractive women almost daily and had no such reaction. Not only attractive women, but friends, women who should stir the kind of response that this one had, but they didn't.

He headed to his kitchen to get a cold beer and get Talia Barton's big blue eyes and million-dollar legs out of his thoughts.

He opened his refrigerator and looked at all the casseroles, desserts and salads the local bachelorettes had brought. He wasn't aware he even knew this many women. With a sigh he retrieved a beer, sat at the table and opened the envelope Talia had given him. He read the notes she'd jotted in her neat teacher's handwriting. Then he called to make an appointment for tomorrow with the DNA people.

He took a long pull on his beer and stared into space, thinking about Regina and little Arthur. He wondered if he would ever stop hurting, ever stop missing them. How was he going to love a little girl he didn't know when longing for Artie and Regina filled his heart?

Artie had been so tiny. Nick had rocked him, talked to him, sang to him, bathed and dressed him and carried him around when he cried. Occasionally, he gave him a bottle, but he hadn't been fully responsible for his son's care, and he never worried about what to do because if he had a question, Regina was there to answer it.

A fourteen-month-old baby girl would be another matter. She needed a mother who would shower her with love. The thought worried him until he shrugged it away. There was no reason to worry until he knew without any doubt that this little child was his.

And if Hattie was his child—how much would that bring Talia into his life?

Two

Talia Barton drove away from Nick Duncan's ranch house. She could barely see for her tears, so she pulled over and tried to get a grip on her emotions. She loved Hattie and felt as if she was a second mother to the little girl. It had hurt terribly to try to get Nick to realize he had a responsibility to take Hattie. She had lived with a chilling panic since people from the state agency had stepped in and said Hattie should be a ward of the state because there was nothing official to indicate the mother had wanted Talia to raise Hattie.

Madeline's life had been filled with joy, excitement and the promise of a glittering future in the music world. She had talked about seeing an attorney and getting papers drawn up to make Talia Hattie's guardian, but hadn't gotten around to it. Madeline had been so busy with her career, so filled with a love of life and her baby, that she hadn't considered anything happening to take that life away. It hadn't occurred to Talia to worry about the possibility, either. The accident had been a painful, numbing shock that still was a raw hurt.

Thinking about parting with Hattie hurt and Talia cried quietly. Finally she dried her eyes. She prayed Nick would want his baby and would come forward to claim her. Talia knew that, whatever happened, she would not get to keep Hattie as her own. She had to accept that. If she couldn't raise Hattie herself, then she wanted the best possible outcome and right now there were only two solutions: Nick Duncan would claim his baby or the state would take Hattie. Talia didn't want the latter to happen.

Thinking about Hattie and wanting to get home to see her, Talia gripped the steering wheel tightly and pulled onto the road.

Her thoughts shifted to Nick and the moment she had first met him. The first time they had touched, the mere handshake had sent tingles radiating through her and made breathing difficult. What shocked her was that he had felt the electricity, too. She'd seen it in the look he gave her, felt it as he took her hand lightly, a slight, impersonal touch, yet it hadn't been impersonal. She had tingled to her toes, and she knew he reacted, as well. Another twist she couldn't worry about. Right now she was focused on getting him to become the dad for Hattie that he truly was, and as soon as possible. Hopefully, Nick would let her stay part of Hattie's life. Was that asking so much?

Yet she didn't know Nick and he didn't know her. What if someday he married again and his wife didn't want Talia in their lives? Would Nick keep Hattie from her?

She didn't want to think what would happen if Nick wouldn't claim Hattie. First he needed proof that he was her dad. The minute she'd seen him, Talia had noticed the family resemblance. Hattie had Nick's green eyes with little flecks of gold, his tangled brown hair and the same facial structure.

Talia shook her head. How was she going to go about work and keep focused on what she needed to do? All she could think about was Hattie every minute. She pulled into the day-care parking lot, climbed out of the car and went inside to find her little charge.

Hattie saw her coming and held out her arms. Talia picked her up, smiling at her and kissing her cheek as she squeezed her close. "Hi, sweetie," she said, smiling at the baby, feeling warmth and love pour over her. She loved this child with all her heart. If only Nick would love Hattie, too. She told herself he would, once he was certain she was his. Surely he wouldn't want the state to take her.

"How's my girl?" she asked, snuggling close and

inhaling the sweet scent of baby powder. Then she leaned back to look at Hattie, who smiled and patted Talia's cheek. "I love you," Talia said.

"Wuv you," Hattie replied softly in her childish voice, but the words thrilled Talia even when it was *wuv* instead of *love*.

"I'm taking you home now," Talia said, getting Hattie's bag, gathering up her other things. She talked to two of the women who ran the day care and then signed out and left with Hattie.

"Once he sees you, I don't see how your daddy can resist you," Talia said as she buckled the child into the car seat.

"Da," Hattie repeated.

"That's right," Talia said, brightening. "Daddy. We'll work on that one. Da-dee," she said, drawing out the word. Hattie giggled.

"I hope he makes you laugh. Da-dee," Talia repeated, hoping Hattie would pick up the sounds and learn the word.

"We'll keep trying. I want your daddy to be unable to resist you. I don't want him to take you from me, but if he doesn't, the state will, so better your daddy, who might let me see you occasionally."

The first week of May, Nick was in his office on the ranch, staring at the document in his hand. The results of the DNA test. Absolute proof that he was Hattie's father. He mulled over the news when Stan knocked and entered the open door.

"I needed to drive into town and thought I'd stop to see you. Are you doing okay with this?"

"That I'm a dad? Hell, no, I'm not." He'd told his brother the DNA test results as soon as they'd arrived. Over the last few hours he'd read them a dozen times. He dropped the report back on his desk. "Talia Barton is bringing Hattie to my Dallas house tomorrow so I can meet her. We're both trying to ease into this. Talia is hurting over losing her charge and I can't imagine becoming a parent to a fourteen-month-old little girl. I don't know how to cope with a baby girl."

Stan stared at him with his brow furrowed as he pushed his hat back on his head. "You want to let the state take her?"

Startled, Nick looked up at his brother, his brows rising.

"Sorry," Stan said. "I know you don't want to do that and I wouldn't want to, either. I'm sorry I even asked you a question like that."

"Forget it. She's mine and I'll take the responsibility that I should, though this deal just tears at me. I didn't even know the mother. I feel like every time I look at that little girl, I'll want her to be Artie."

"Sorry, Nick. You'll get used to her. I'll help any way I can."

Nick heard the earnest note in his brother's voice and he smiled. "Thanks, Stan. That offer means a lot," he said, suddenly feeling proud of his younger brother for volunteering to help.

"I've got to run. I just stopped for a minute. When tomorrow is Ms. Barton coming to see you and bringing the baby?"

"In the afternoon. In the morning I'll go to Dallas and she'll bring Hattie by after her last class."

"You're a dad and I'm an uncle to a baby girl. Wow. That does take some getting used to." His wistful look was replaced by a serious one. "I'm surprised the state hasn't already stepped in and taken the baby from Ms. Barton. She doesn't have legal rights."

"She's a teacher in a community college and she has a quiet, take-charge manner that probably makes people do what she wants."

"A battle-ax?"

Smiling, Nick shook his head. "Trust me, you'll never use those words again after you see her."

"A hottie?"

"She's stunning. You'll see. In addition, she has that authoritative manner, in a quieter way, that our grandmother does."

"No kidding. I can't wait to meet her."

Nick didn't reply, but he looked forward to seeing her again himself and that shocked him. He didn't want to have that reaction to her because she had upended his life.

He walked out with Stan. "I don't want to tell Grandmother until I have everything lined up. I don't want her trying to move into my house."

"What a thought. Of course, if you let Grandmother move in, you won't ever have to make another decision. You can just drift."

"You know better than that. She'd make all the decisions but she'd keep me hopping every second. No, she doesn't know until I'm ready. You go ahead and tell Blake and Adam and I'll call them or text." He knew he'd have better luck with his other two brothers than his grandmother.

"Good deal."

"Talia said Hattie looks like me. We'll see."

Stan shot him a horrified look. "I'm afraid I can't imagine a little baby girl looking like you." Then he smiled.

"Frankly, I can't, either," Nick said, running his hand over the brown stubble on his jaw.

"Even if you try to keep her out of your hair, Grandmother will want to approve of the nanny you hire. And I'm sure you're hiring a nanny."

"I don't know what I'll do." Nick couldn't stop his fears from surfacing again. He'd been fighting them for the last few hours. "I don't even know this little girl, much less love her. I keep thinking how she won't have anyone who loves her here. Talia Barton adores her. She'll go from having love poured out to her to a bunch of strangers. That's not good and it's worrying me."

"We're not a bunch of ogres, Nick, but I see what you mean. She'll need someone to love her. It may not help her disposition, either," Stan said.

Nick had already thought of that, but he was more worried about having a little baby who wasn't loved.

"If she's that good-looking, marry this Talia person," Stan said, breaking into his thoughts.

"Stan!" Nick said, annoyed and amused at the same time.

"I'm kidding. I wouldn't worry, Nick. Babies adapt and we'll all be here to help. You know Grandmother is going to love this baby. She adored Artie. And pretty soon, we'll all love her, too."

"You're right, I suppose. Grandmother is going to have to cooperate on this one. I can't deal with a hassle from her."

"Send me a picture of the teacher," Stan said, going down the porch steps. He glanced over his shoulder. "I might want to propose. Then I'd be daddy and uncle to your little girl." He laughed at his own joke and Nick shook his head.

"You're hopeless, Stan. Take your suggestions and go," Nick said, laughing with his brother.

"Seriously, I'll help if you need me, although I don't know as much about babies as you do. My expertise ends with colts and calves."

"Thanks, Stan," Nick said, feeling a bond with his brother.

As Stan drove away, Nick returned to his office, but he couldn't get his mind to focus on the ranch work in front of him. He remembered Madeline. Since meeting Talia, he recalled everything about that night. He was sure he had used protection, yet here was this little baby and the DNA definitely made her *his* baby. He couldn't get accustomed to the idea, and guilt swamped him at the thought he would have to take her away from someone who poured out love to her and place her in a family of strangers.

Enough, he told himself. It'd work out. It had to.

He picked up the leather-bound ledger but the figures swam before his eyes. All he could think about was his new status as a daddy…and his electrifying attraction to Talia Barton.

Late the following sunny May afternoon Nick paced back and forth. He was in his mansion in a gated community of Dallas, waiting for Talia to arrive, and then he would meet his daughter. That still didn't seem possible. A night at a party—when he'd had too much to drink, been too long alone, hurting over his loss and trying to overcome the grief and desperation he felt—he'd had sex with a woman he'd barely known. Now he had a daughter for the rest of his life. A little girl who was going to move in with a father who was a total stranger. He knew that was better than the state and they would probably all grow to love her, but it was going to be rough for the little girl for a time and he hated that. And it was breaking Talia's heart, something he could understand all too well because of the loss of his son.

When he heard a car, he glanced at his watch. Talia was on time. He thought about seeing her again and that was one bit of this whole thing that he looked forward to, even though he shouldn't because she had already complicated his life beyond measure.

He hurried to the front door. When he reached for the door, he glanced out and saw Talia coming up the walk carrying a little girl in her arms. His pulse jumped as his glance swept over Talia's high heels and her deep blue sleeveless dress. Her hair was high, pinned on the sides of her head, and fell in spiral curls over her shoulders. The curls bounced slightly with each step she took. His gaze shifted to the baby in her arms. The little girl had one thin arm on Talia's shoulder with her fingers wound in Talia's long curls. Her other arm hung at her side. She had wispy, tangled brown hair, and from a distance she looked like a pretty child. He couldn't imagine that this was his baby, but she was. It was a shock each time he thought about it, and seeing her didn't make it any more real to him.

A little girl he didn't know in the arms of a woman he would like to know if circumstances were different. His life was going to change forever and he couldn't even imagine how.

He opened the door. "Come in. You and Hattie."

"Thank you," Talia said in a tight voice. From the sound of it, he was sure she was hurting. If she felt this bad just introducing him to his daughter, how much worse was it going to get for her?

He looked down at the baby in her arms, gaz-

ing into wide green eyes with gold flecks that were
like his own and ran in his family. Hattie had the
same color hair he did, the same facial features, but
slightly darker skin. As if sensing something was
wrong with the adults around her, she gazed solemnly up at him.

He stepped back so Talia could enter and closed
the door behind her, catching up with them, his gaze
lingering briefly on the sexy sway of Talia's hips as
she walked. Hattie twisted around to stare at him,
studying him intently.

"Let's go to the family room. It's probably the
most childproof room in the house. Arthur wasn't
toddling around or even crawling, so we didn't get
anything ready for a baby to explore."

"I'll watch her and she'll go home with me until
you're ready to take her," Talia said. "Unless you
have other plans."

"Plans? I'm just trying to get a grip on my new
status."

She glanced up with worry in her big eyes.

"You're worrying about me taking her from you,"
he said.

She shook her head. "I'm worrying you won't
take her and the state will get her."

He caught Talia's arm lightly, instantly having
that startling awareness from the physical contact.
He heard her breath catch and realized she felt something, too. Why did sparks fly between them when
they didn't even know each other? Looking intently

at her, he released her just as quickly. Standing so close, he was acutely aware of her while he tried to focus on the problem.

"Let's settle that one right now. I have the DNA and Hattie is my baby. I'm not giving my baby to the state to try to place in foster homes or wherever they can find. I'll take Hattie and you'll get to see her. You have my promise," he said, emotions tearing at him because he was making a huge commitment that he didn't even know if he could live up to. He had been tossed into fatherhood abruptly and it brought back memories of his baby boy and of his wife, of being in love and happy and filled with plans for a future that vanished in a crushing blow when their private plane went down in a storm. He hadn't ever expected to raise a little girl he didn't even know, a child born to a mother he was with for only a few hours. As he looked down into Talia's wide, frightened eyes, his insides churned and he wondered if he could possibly keep the promise he was making to her. This promise was monumental and a life-changer. Along with tremendous responsibility, it brought heartache. Every time he looked at this child he'd be reminded of what he had lost in the past.

As she searched his gaze, tears filled Talia's eyes. She brushed away her tears hastily. "You really mean that, don't you?" she asked softly.

"Yes, I do," he said. "Don't cry. I'll take Hattie

because she's my child and you'll get to see her. We'll figure something out."

"I wanted so badly to adopt her and be her mother. My attorney said I'd have to go through the state to apply." Shaking her head, Talia turned away, carrying the baby to the window and talking softly to her. He let her go so she could get herself pulled together while he tried to calm his own nerves.

A few minutes later he glanced around and saw Talia was standing a few feet behind him, holding out Hattie to place her in his arms. As their hands brushed, he felt a frisson of electricity shoot up his arm. He inhaled her perfume, an enticing scent. As he took Hattie, his gaze met Talia's, and if he let himself, he could drown in the blue depths of her eyes.

His heart pounding, he forced himself to step back slightly, and his gaze was captured by the baby, who stared at him with huge eyes.

She was soft, warm and smelled of soap and lotion. She wore a white blouse and a pink jumper.

"Hi, Hattie," he said quietly.

She touched a button on his shirt and then touched his chin.

He felt little fingers moving over the stubble on his chin while he gazed at her as solemnly as she looked at him. She ran her tiny fingers over his face. "I'll contact the state human services and let them know that I have my baby. I think that will take her name off any list they have."

"It will as soon as you've notified them that

you're taking her permanently. My attorney checked and I can't just come calling and then take her home with me. I have a friend who is an attorney and he's been keeping up with this. When you step in and actually take care of her and she lives with you, they have to back off and leave you alone unless they get a complaint about the way she's being raised, which they won't. Since Madeline's death, Hattie hasn't had any family except me. There's no one else who cares about her except the women at the day care. They think she's sweet and adorable."

"So except for those ladies, you're her whole world. We'll definitely have to work something out so you can come see her."

Her blue eyes widened and he saw hope blossom in them. Then she turned them to the child he held.

"Hattie, this is your daddy. Daddy," she repeated distinctly and looked at Nick. He looked down at her, and for a few seconds all he could think about was Talia and how close she stood, how tempting she smelled. She looked back at Hattie. "Daddy," Talia repeated.

"Da," Hattie said, running her fingers on Nick's jaw again.

"God love the little children," Nick said softly and turned away. Emotions tore at him when she ran her tiny fingers over his chin because Hattie made him think about Artie. He would never hear Artie say "Daddy," and it hurt. He missed his son and felt conflicted over the little girl in his arms. He pulled out his handkerchief and wiped away tears, trying to get a better grip on his emotions.

"Do you want me to take her?" Talia asked.

"No. I'll pull myself together. Sometimes it just hits me out of the blue and I miss Artie."

"That's the way I'm going to feel about Hattie," Talia said so softly, he didn't think she was even talking to him.

He heard her and knew she was right, and that disturbed him. "At least you can come visit and I'll let her visit you," he said, making another commitment that might be difficult.

Hattie's little fingers ran over his cheek, her mouth turned down, and she looked worried by his tears. He smiled at her and she stared for a few seconds and then smiled.

"Da," she repeated. He looked into her big green eyes and they stared at each other. Could he be a real dad to her? Would he grow to love her the way he had loved Artie? Right now, he felt at a loss and he hurt. Guilt rocked him for missing Artie each time he looked at Hattie. It wasn't right, but he couldn't help himself because he longed for his little son. Hattie was a little girl he didn't know.

"One thing's for sure," he said. "She's related to me. She has the Duncan hair and eyes. I'm glad I have the DNA results, but this child is a Duncan."

Holding Hattie, Nick walked across the room with her. He wasn't sure what to do next. At a store specializing in babies, he had bought a small stuffed pink bunny for Hattie. The bunny was in a gift sack with pink tissue paper covering it and he had placed it on a game table.

He picked up the small sack and held it in front of her. "Hattie, this is for you from me. It's your present," he said quietly.

She looked up at him and then down at the sack. He held it closer in front of her. "This is for you."

She looked at the sack and at him in uncertainty, but then she pulled one of the pieces of tissue paper. As it came out of the sack, Nick smiled encouragement. "A bunny."

"Bun," she repeated and retrieved the small pink stuffed rabbit. He took the sack from her to set it on a table. "Mine," she said, hugging the bunny, making him smile.

"That was sweet, Nick," Talia said softly. "She likes you. She hasn't protested going to you or wanted me to take her. That's good."

He walked to Talia and held out Hattie. "I'll give her to you."

"Of course," she said, taking Hattie from him, their hands and arms brushing and bringing that same electric awareness of touching Talia that he felt each time they had contact. He glanced at her as he stood so close and she looked up, their gazes meeting. For another moment he was more aware of Talia than of Hattie. He couldn't understand the physical attraction, especially at a time when they both were torn up emotionally.

Moving away, he didn't want to pursue the feelings she stirred. His life was tangled enough already and he didn't need one more emotional pull. He suspected she wasn't any more enthused about the sparks flying between them than he was, but he couldn't figure how there could be one little glimmer of appeal under their current circumstances. She had brought him a monumental problem, changing his life, demolishing the little calm and peace he was beginning to get back after losing Regina and Artie. Talia was awakening feelings he hadn't experienced in a long time and he wasn't ready to deal with them. He didn't want to complicate his life with Talia as well as Hattie. Hattie was all he could deal with at present. A baby girl who needed two loving parents and siblings, but that wasn't possible.

He stared at her and thought about Stan telling him to marry Talia. "My brothers are filled with curiosity and eventually I'll have to tell my grandmother."

Talia's expression changed and she looked stricken. "You don't think your grandmother will like Hattie?"

"Talia, relax," he said patiently. "My brothers will be in awe because they're uncles now. My grandmother likes babies and was devastated by the loss of Regina and Artie. The reason I said I'd tell her eventually is because my grandmother is a take-charge person and she will be all over me with ideas about what I need to do. I can handle that, but it's tedious because I don't want to hurt her feelings."

Talia ran her hand across her forehead. "I know your mother is deceased and your dad lives in Palm Beach. You're the oldest son at thirty-four. Your brother Stan is thirty-three, Adam is thirty-one, and the youngest, Blake, is twenty-nine. Your dad started Duncan Energy. You took over later and then stepped down, and Adam is CEO. Blake works for him while you, as well as Stan, are on the board."

Startled, he looked up again. "How do you know all that?"

"I hired a PI to find out about you before I contacted you. I'm sorry that I pried into your life but I wanted to know what kind of person I would be dealing with."

He nodded. "I don't blame you. My dad will have no interest in Hattie one way or another. He's into his own life and we don't see him. He was a good dad and we loved him and everything was fine until Mom died when I was sixteen. Dad never has recovered. He drinks and he's married to his fifth wife. He doesn't come home to Texas, and when he does come back, my grandmother ties into him. She's my maternal grandmother and those two don't get along."

"I'm sorry. I don't have family, so family seems special and important to me, something valuable to be cherished."

He nodded. "That's a good outlook."

She blushed. "Well, again, I'm sorry for prying into your life. By the way, I know your age, so if you want to know mine, I'm twenty-nine. Madeline was twenty-eight when she was killed in the car wreck."

"She was beautiful and talented. I remember that much. Talia, forget hiring a PI. You had a good reason. That's how you found my attorney, isn't it?"

"Yes," she admitted.

"I wondered." Hattie chose that moment to let out a shrill giggle as she played with her bunny, eliciting a smile from Nick. "She is a happy little girl, isn't she?"

Talia put the baby on the floor so she could play. "She's a sweetheart. She's had a big loss in her life but she's still happy. I've tried to make up for the loss of her mother as best I can, which just means being there for her and showering her with love."

"You've done a good job and I'm grateful." He looked at Talia again. Her long blond curls framed her face and he realized he could spend the day looking at her. His gaze lowered to her mouth and he wondered what it would be like to kiss her. When he realized the drift of his thoughts, he tried to shift his focus. He reached down and ruffled Hattie's brown hair, which earned another giggle.

"She's been around a lot of kids at the day care and her mother used to take her to music tryouts and rehearsals," Talia said, "so she's comfortable with people. You'll see."

"Artie was happy, too. He was so easy."

Hattie was busy with her new bunny, making sounds as she played with it. She was a beautiful baby but he couldn't feel like she was his yet. Nor could he keep from wanting Artie and Regina.

Talia watched Hattie, another of those concerned looks on her face. He knew what she was thinking about—that moment when she would have to give up little Hattie, when she would have to hand her over to Nick forever. He ached for her because he knew how she felt. He missed his own little boy, the baby he had rocked, kissed, fed and held. Hattie and Talia were bringing back memories that ripped him apart.

"Aw, hell, Talia, this is tearing us both up," he said, turning to her. "Let's figure where we'll go from here, what we'll do next and get this over with. I have to take her, but not today. We'll continue to send her to day care until we work out what we'll do. Then I'll take Hattie, so the state will have to back off and get the hell out of our lives."

He glanced at the child. "Thank goodness she doesn't know what's going on. She's going to miss you like hell." Talia had become mama to her. When they loved each other, a mother and child formed the tightest possible bond. Nick rubbed his forehead as he thought about what he was doing—taking a baby from the only mother she now knew. When Hattie woke crying in the night and he came to comfort her, would she be scared?

He looked intently at Talia and she stared at him. "What?" she asked. "What's wrong?"

"As far as she knows now, you're her mother," he said.

"Yes, but you'll be her daddy before you know it," Talia answered solemnly. "And suddenly you'll be a family. You're bound to marry again and then she'll have a mama who loves her."

Talia looked away and he knew she was fighting tears again and he couldn't blame her.

He barely knew her, yet he ached for her. He wanted to put his arms around her and try to comfort her and to calm his own nerves and feelings of loss, but they had a fiery chemistry between them that he didn't want to ignite. He didn't know why sparks flared when they touched, but he didn't want the physical attraction to escalate. He didn't need that to complicate his thinking. He had to avoid crossing a line where they had more emotional problems between them to deal with, but it was a strain to keep from reaching out and comforting her. He fought the urge and stood facing her as he said, "Talia, you should raise her."

She turned her back to him and he suspected she lost the battle to try to avoid crying. "That was my biggest fantasy, that I was a stay-at-home mom and with her every day," she said in a soft voice as if talking to herself. After a moment she wiped her eyes while her back was still turned. "This is hard, Nick. It hurts because I love her as if she was my own baby. I've had two miscarriages, so I've lost two babies and I'm going to lose another one now—one that I love with all my heart."

This time he couldn't keep from stepping up close to her to pat her on the shoulder, and even that touch just made him want to pull her into his arms and hold her. "Shh, Talia," he whispered. He looked at the baby seated on the floor, still playing with her new bunny. She looked up at him and smiled, holding out her arms.

"Talia, she wants to be picked up," he said.

Glancing over her shoulder, Talia moved instantly, wiping away tears as she turned to get Hattie before he did. She scooped her into her arms and held her, hugging her and kissing her cheek. Hattie smiled and held Talia.

And Nick hurt for them and for himself.

Talia sat on the floor with her, doubling her long legs under her. He couldn't keep from letting his gaze sweep over her gorgeous, long shapely legs. As he watched them play, he couldn't deny his attraction. She was a beautiful woman.

Again, he thought Talia knew how to take care of Hattie better than anyone else on earth.

She stood and faced him while Hattie curled up on the floor and played with her bunny.

"She's getting sleepy, so we should go. You've got your DNA results and you've met your baby girl. I'll take her home with me tonight. You plan what you'll do, get baby equipment—and I will be happy to help with any or all of that if you want me to—and then

I'll turn Hattie over to you. It really shouldn't take you long. I can give you a list of baby furniture she'll need. I don't want to give mine up because I hope you'll let her stay with me sometimes."

"Of course she can stay with you. She can stay a lot. Talia, she'll be lost without you," he said.

"She'll adapt. Children do adapt," she said and he heard the strain in her voice. "Whatever help you need, let me know."

"I'm letting you know right now," he said, suddenly wanting her help and knowing Hattie needed someone who loved her to be with her. If this were Artie, Nick absolutely wouldn't want him handed over to a house of strangers. Talia was the one person Hattie would know and love. And who would love Hattie with all her heart in return. Babies thrived on love. Talia would be the most possible help because she was already parenting Hattie.

The thought struck him like a lightning bolt. Suddenly he knew exactly what he had to do.

"I need your help," he said. "Move in here while we work this out. You don't have to tonight, but soon. I can have someone drive you to school and pick up you and Hattie."

"In a limo?" she said, smiling and shaking her head. "I'm almost tempted to answer yes just to see everyone's reactions. I would be the most famous person in the school. No, Nick, thanks. I can't move in with you. We'll get this over and done with without me moving in because all too soon, I'd have to move out again. I'd cry over her every day."

"Okay. Come over for dinner tomorrow night, bring Hattie, and I'll have my first questions and problems lined up. And I will need the list of baby furniture. I got rid of the baby furniture that I had because I couldn't see any point in keeping it."

"If you want me to go shopping with you, I will."

He looked into wide eyes that made him momentarily forget baby furniture. "I won't go shopping," he said. "I'll hire someone to buy everything. You can earn some money on the side if you want to do it."

"I'll get it but you don't have to pay me. Just pay for the furniture. Where do you want it delivered? Here or the ranch?"

"I'll need it at both places. I live here and I live there. She's so little and yet she needs enough things to fill a big truck." He let out a deep sigh. "I need a wife."

"I'm sure you can find a wife easily enough," she said. "But please get one who really likes Hattie and means what she says."

He meant his comment as a joke, but he saw the sincerity in Talia's eyes. They were filled with worry and he was part of the problem. He stepped close, placing his hands on her shoulders, feeling her warm, smooth skin where her dress was sleeveless.

"I can't tell you to stop worrying because I know this hurts, but you'll always get to see Hattie. You'll get to be with her. She isn't going out of your life. Hang on to that. I'd give anything if I could see Artie."

She blinked and her eyebrows arched. "Oh, Nick. I'm sorry. I've probably been making things worse for you."

"We both hurt."

"Just love Hattie. She's going to need your love. She lost her mother, never knew her grandparents and now she's losing me. She'll need your love."

Her eyes filled with tears. "Sorry, Nick, sometimes I just can't avoid crying. I love her so much."

"I understand. I'll love her because she's my child. I only knew Artie two months, but I loved him beyond measure," he said so quietly, he didn't know whether she heard, but it didn't matter.

"There's just no way I can be her mother in the eyes of the state," Talia said, looking at Hattie. "Love doesn't even fit into their equation." Talia looked up to find Nick studying her intently.

He gazed at her in silence so long that she focused on him, frowning when she studied him. "What, Nick? What's wrong?"

Lost in his thoughts, he blinked. "I'm thinking. There's one way you can become her mother as far as the state is concerned. It would be legal and binding."

Frowning, she shook her head. "I don't think so.

We don't have any—" She broke off to stare at him while her frown deepened.

"We can marry," he said.

Three

"Excuse me—did I hear you propose marriage?" she asked, her heart thumping wildly. "Did you just propose to me?" Shocked, she stared at him and he gazed steadily back.

"Yes, I did," he replied, sounding surprised, as if he were telling himself as well as her.

"Oh, my heavens." Her head swam and she gulped for breath while she stared at him. "I may faint. I'm not going to," she added hastily. "I've never fainted."

"Hattie needs someone with her who loves her. I'm a stranger and so is my whole family. Anyone I'd hire would be even less concerned with her welfare. You love her and shower her with love and she loves you. Hattie needs someone to love her. You and I can have a marriage of convenience."

Talia couldn't believe what she was hearing. She would get to be with Hattie. She turned to look at the baby playing on the floor. She would get to be Hattie's real mother. "Nick, if we married, I could adopt Hattie. She would really be my baby, my daughter. Actually, our baby." Her hands flew to her chest. "I feel as if I'm in a dream. A dream come true. Do you really mean that? You're actually proposing marriage?"

"A marriage of convenience. We'll both benefit. I know we're not in love. I can't love again and we don't even know each other. But it'd be a legal marriage to keep Hattie happy and help us both out." He grasped her hands and asked her again. "Will you marry me in a marriage of convenience?"

"I don't think you know what you're doing, Nick. How happy I am." Excitement made her shake. "I can adopt her legally and Hattie would really be my little girl."

"That's right. You could adopt her."

She held back a gasp when it finally all sank in. "But you're right, Nick. We don't even know each other. Are you sure?"

"Yes, I am," he said quietly, looking as if he was still giving it thought.

"Nick," she gushed and stepped closer to throw her arms around him.

He caught her, slipping one strong arm around her waist while he laughed softly.

Smiling at him, she felt light-headed and giddy. "Oh, my. You just made my biggest, deepest wish come true—to get to be Hattie's legal mother. I get to watch her grow up. You just gave me the world." She leaned back to look at him, gazing into green eyes that hid whatever he was thinking or feeling. Then she hugged him tightly.

"So… I take it your answer is—"

She stepped back to laugh. "Yes. My answer is yes. I'll marry you, Nick Duncan."

"You do realize I mean a legal marriage, but not a real marriage. That wasn't what I had in mind," he said. "You've heard of a marriage of convenience, right?" He didn't wait for her response. "We can marry and work out how we'll live. If we marry legally, the state can't touch us and you can legally adopt Hattie."

"I understand, Nick. Your proposal is still a dream come true. I love Hattie more than anyone or anything else and you are enabling me to keep her, to raise her, to love her and be with her. You have my forever thanks."

"There's no need to thank me," he said. "We'll be helping each other out." He gestured to the sofa and they both sat. "You'll have to get me up-to-date about your life and your history. You seem to know mine sufficiently."

That part was true, she silently acknowledged.

She stared at him. She could easily see that Nick Duncan was a sexy, good-looking man, but her research had told her a lot about him. He was a billionaire oilman, rancher, widower with three brothers. He had a father he rarely saw and a grandmother living on his ranch. The Duncans were part of Texas history because it was a generations-old ranching family with immense wealth and political influence partially because his great-grandfather had been in the Texas Senate.

And here he was, offering her a marriage of convenience.

She looked at Hattie and couldn't get her breath. She hadn't imagined there was any way on earth to get to keep Hattie, and yet Nick was holding one out to her. While she couldn't imagine marrying a man she didn't know, that was what she was going to do. But she wasn't worried. The PI hadn't turned up anything bad about Nick. If she married him, she would always have Hattie. She could barely think beyond that point. She would become Hattie's legal mother, and as long as they both lived, Hattie would be part of her life.

Her gaze went from Hattie to Nick and she was suddenly overwhelmed by emotion. "Nick—" She broke off, placing her hands over her face.

In seconds, she felt his hands on her upper arms, gently holding her. "Talia, don't cry."

"I can't keep from it. I'm sorry. It's just so overwhelming." She fumbled in a pocket to pull out a dainty handkerchief and wipe her eyes.

"Talia, if you need them, I can give you references. I promise you, I'm a good guy. I—"

She looked up at Nick, her brows knitted. Why was he talking about references? Then it hit her, and she smiled. "I don't need references, Nick. I'm crying for joy. Because it's too miraculous to be possible that I might get to keep Hattie."

"Oh." He smiled sheepishly.

"You just thought that up, didn't you? The whole marriage-of-convenience idea."

"Yes, but the more I think about it, the more I think it will work." He stood up, walked to Hattie and picked her up.

"Talia, this is my child. I don't want to take her from someone she loves and trusts and thrust her into a houseful of strangers, most of us men. She needs a loving mother. I couldn't bear to have had Artie put into a home of strangers. She's only fourteen months old and I know she'll adjust, but if we marry, she will go right along being the happy little child she is and she won't have a big adjustment to make. I'll have someone I think I'll like to love and take care of Hattie and help me raise her. And you'll be with Hattie and be her legal mother."

Her thoughts swirled and she looked at Hattie in the crook of his arm, which looked so natural.

Nick sat with her on his lap and Hattie immediately climbed down. Holding to his knee, she reached for a small table and then moved to plop down on the floor in front of a brass box filled with magazines. Hattie pulled one out to toss it behind her and Talia hurried toward her.

"Let her play with the magazines unless she'll get paper cuts," Nick said. "She's not going to hurt anything in that box. Those magazines will be recycled whenever Tina and her cleaning crew get to them."

"Cleaning crew, a limo, two mansions... Nick, I don't have that kind of life." Under normal circumstances she didn't think it would ever work out between her and someone like Nick. But this was a marriage of convenience. "But I can't get beyond the realization that now I get to keep Hattie and I'll become her mother. I can hardly sit still. I feel like dancing around the room. I feel as if I could dance all night and shout for joy."

He smiled. "I'm glad. I think this will be good for both of us. It lifts a ton of worries off my shoulders."

She sat down beside him. "The biggest thing is that we don't know each other at all."

"We'll get to know each other and you can adjust to the other stuff. Riding in a limo is not that different from riding in a car," he added and she shook her head. He sat back, placing one booted foot on his knee. He looked handsome, sexy, strong, and she realized she could easily fall in love with him, but he would never love her in return. They already had lightning streaking between them if they barely touched. How could she marry him, be around him constantly and keep from falling in love? She didn't think he ever would because all he had talked about since she met him was how much he missed his wife and baby. Was she willing to risk falling in love with him to get to be Hattie's mother? That was her fantasy, and now it was coming true. Yes, falling in love with Nick was worth the risk.

"Why don't you tell me about yourself," he suggested.

"I've had a very ordinary life in many ways. I don't have much family. I'm an only child and my mother died of breast cancer when I was a freshman in college. My father died suddenly from a heart attack when I was fifteen. He had insurance and he'd had a good job in the insurance business, so I was financially okay. I invested most of my inheritance and have done pretty well with it. I went to college on part of it, and I had scholarships for the rest of it." She stopped and stared at him. "I can't believe we're doing this, Nick."

"Go ahead. Tell me more about yourself."

She stared at him a moment, shrugged and continued, "I've always wanted to be a teacher. I love art and I like teaching. My senior year in college I married. His parents had money and provided generously for us. We were seniors, had money and neither of us worked. When we graduated, he still didn't want me to work. He looked for a job, but it was a half-hearted hunt while he played golf and hung out at the country club."

"Who was he?"

"Quinton Smith from Houston."

Nick shook his head. "Not any family I know."

"Quinton is one of the reasons I hired a PI to check on you. Quinton was wealthy and he let it make a mess of his life, to my way of thinking. You're wealthy and I wanted to know you weren't anything like him. I also wanted to know some other things about you before I turned Hattie over to you."

"I don't mind the PI. I don't blame you. Go on about your life."

"Quinton couldn't find a job he liked and I never knew if he really got offers or not. After my first miscarriage I discovered that he didn't want children while I did. Also, I thought he should get a job. His mother provided abundantly for us and he didn't really see any reason to work if he didn't have to. By that time we were having arguments over his unemployment, and then I got pregnant again. When I miscarried the second time, I wanted a divorce and he did, too. The doctors couldn't find anything wrong. They said the stress was getting to me. Even so, I don't expect to ever have any children of my own. Does that matter to you?"

"No. You and I won't have a regular marriage. After I lost Artie I didn't expect to have any more children. Now I do have another child. That's enough. Under the circumstances, I don't want another child now. Can you accept that?"

"Of course. With my track record for miscarriages, I don't think I could give you any if you wanted more children. And I agree that children should come into a home filled with love. By the way, while I was in college with all the bills paid, I got my master's degree, so I'm qualified to teach in some colleges."

"You won't be teaching, Talia. I want you home with Hattie."

"Oh, Nick, that's my dream. I never, ever expected it to happen."

They were silent a moment and she returned to what she had been saying to him. "I only knew my husband two months before we married," she said, watching Hattie toss magazines behind her as she steadily removed them from the box. "I rushed into that marriage." She looked up at Nick. "I'm rushing into this marriage of convenience, too."

"This is different. We're not in love and we don't know each other. This is for convenience to get what we both want," he said. "Talia, if it doesn't work out and we get a divorce, you'll be Hattie's mother and we'll legally work it out to share her. As soon as we're married, you can start the adoption process so she will legally be your daughter. Is there anything else about your life, your past, I should know?"

Smiling at him, she shook her head. "No. I've led a quiet, uneventful life. You've heard all the highlights. I've told you about being friends with Madeline." Her gaze fluttered over him. And then it hit her. The handsome rancher facing her was going to marry her. Her heartbeat raced and she couldn't stop smiling. She would be a stay-at-home mother to Hattie, and she would be married to one of the most handsome, appealing men she had ever met. A man who had proposed for his baby's sake. That almost made her fall in love with him right then and there.

"Not that I need to know now, but I'm curious," she said when she gathered her thoughts. "Where will she go to school?"

He smiled and her heart fluttered again. How was she going to guard her heart against a smile like that? Against a body like his? She took a deep breath and released it slowly.

"You can move back to Dallas if you want her in school here. Otherwise, there is a country school she can attend if she lives on the ranch. My brothers and I went there. It's a good school. But that's in the future. Looking at the present, we'll need to child-proof some rooms, keep her out of others until she understands the rules."

"The first thing I'd like to see you do is put a fence around that swimming pool."

"I'll get on it tomorrow. Also, tomorrow we can get an alarm that will go off if anyone falls into the pool."

Her gaze swept the large, casual family room with a game table on one side of the room, floor-to-ceiling sliding glass doors along the side opening to the patio and affording a view of his sparkling aqua pool with a waterfall and a fountain. The contemporary room

held glass-and-steel tables and furniture in muted
shades of brown to white. The room was two-story,
with stairs on either side winding to the second level,
where three walls of glass provided panoramic views.
It was a stunning room, but the others on the ground
floor that she had glimpsed through open doors had
been equally impressive. Some had high-beamed
ceilings with marble columns. Others had French
eighteenth-century-style furniture with elegant an-
tique satin and silk finishes. Oil paintings in gilded
frames were on many walls. As she looked around,
she realized that when she became Mrs. Nick Duncan, she would live in this mansion with Hattie. She
couldn't imagine that would be possible. Even more
impossible to imagine, she would live here with Nick.

"Talia?"

She realized she was lost in thoughts about his
proposal and him. "Sorry, Nick. This is all so fantastic. I keep getting carried away by the wonder
of becoming Hattie's mother. What were we discussing? Oh, I remember. Childproofing the house.
You'll need gates for the stairs, of course, and some
things will have to be put away. This contemporary
furniture looks durable and has no sharp corners…
I'm assuming it's all unbreakable glass?"

He nodded. "See, you can deal with all that because you know what needs to be done. I haven't
taken care of a toddler. Artie was a tiny baby."

"It doesn't take long to learn how to childproof
a room."

"There's something else I have to do. I need to set up trusts for you and for Hattie."

"Nick, I have savings. As I said, my dad was in insurance and he had a big policy on Mom and on himself. I've got that money. I live a simple life and I've invested the insurance money. I don't need anything from you."

He looked amused. "You are one in a million, Talia, in a lot of ways. But I'd like to set up trusts for you and Hattie in case something happens to me. If you don't need or want yours, save it for Hattie."

"That's sweet, Nick, and if you want to do that, go ahead. But you've already given me my biggest wish."

"Speaking of Hattie, for now I'd like you to stay on the ranch most of the time. I really would like for us to be a family to whatever extent we could work it out. That would be the best thing for Hattie."

He was sitting there facing her, calmly fulfilling all her dreams and fantasies. She couldn't sit still any longer. "Ahh, Nick," she cried, standing up and flinging her arms in the air. "I can't sit still. It's the most fantastic thing possible. A stay-at-home mom on the ranch. You want us to be a family. It's wonderful."

He let out a laugh as he came to his feet. "You love her so much, Talia, I think this will work and we'll all be happy. A huge worry has lifted from me."

Overjoyed, Talia spun on her heels, but she must

have slipped on one of the glossy magazines because the next thing she knew, Nick was steadying her, his hands on her waist. Instantly, she felt their heat singeing her through her clothes. She looked down at them, then up at him.

She expected him to pull his hands back, but he didn't. He just stood there, looking at her. For a moment, she had to admit she wished he'd never stop touching her. Then she realized the danger zone she was stepping into.

"I—I guess I should take Hattie home now and think about all we've talked about."

Was it her imagination, or did Nick actually look disappointed? He lowered his hands and stepped aside. "Okay." But before she could move, he reached out and grabbed her hand. "Talia, I think this is the best solution for all three of us."

That, she believed with all her heart. But as she looked into his green eyes, so like Hattie's only far more unfathomable, there was another part of her that acknowledged the danger in their plan. And it all started with the sexy man standing in front of her.

"I can't imagine marrying for convenience with love not any part of the equation, but I'll try my best to make it work." Had she really uttered those words, or had she merely thought them in her mind?

"It might not be easy, but nothing worthwhile is ever easy."

"What about having sex?" she asked, feeling heat flood her cheeks the minute the question was out.

His hand left hers and traveled up her arm in a slow, tantalizing path. His eyes blazed the trail till he looked up at her again and something flickered in their depths. Her heart pounded.

"Well, there's one way to find out," he said and slipped his arm around her waist, drawing her against him.

Her hands flew to his muscled arms as she looked into his eyes, and her heart thudded when she saw his intention. What she saw in his expression was personal, hot and demanding. That sizzling reaction they'd had each time there had been the barest physical contact sparked between them while awareness and desire ignited. Her lips tingled and her gaze shifted to his mouth and then she looked into his eyes again. When she did, she received a look that sent a tremor from her head to her toes. He intended to kiss her and she wanted him to.

His arms tightened around her, drawing her flush against his hard, muscled body, a masculine body that caused wild desire to shoot through her. Holding her tightly in his strong arms, he leaned closer and closer, until she yearned for his kiss. When his lips finally met hers, she was consumed by his dazzling kiss. A kiss like none she had ever experienced before. His kiss made her tremble as she wrapped her arms around him and opened her mouth to him, pouring herself, all her joy and excitement and enthusiasm, into her response.

A primal need enveloped her, and she wanted

more of him, more than a kiss, no matter how passionate. His mouth stirred an irresistible, sizzling
longing within her that she knew only hours in his
bed would satisfy. She didn't know if her reaction
was because of his fantastic marriage proposal or
because he was the sexiest man she had ever met
or if it was the fiery, spontaneous reaction they had
to each other.

Now she was dazzled, tingling and wanting him.
From mouth to thighs, her body was pressed against
his. She felt his big Western belt buckle against her,
but it was his lips and tongue that drew her attention. Touching, stroking in a demanding, passionate kiss that made her shake with need. With an
effort, she broke away slightly, staring at him in
shock. She wanted to wrap her arms around him
and continue kissing him, while at the same time,
she was stunned by her response to him. A fleeting
thought made her wonder if she would ever see him
the same way again.

"I think that kiss just answered your question,"
he said in a husky voice, looking intently at her. "I
think we'll do all right together," he added. "And
I'm sure sex will be part of the equation. I'm about
to go up in flames," he added in a husky voice as he
ran his hand across his brow that was beaded with
sweat. They both were gasping for breath.

She barely heard him and it took a second to remember her question. *What about having sex?* Her
pulse still raced and her mouth tingled; every inch

down to her toes throbbed with desire. She had never been kissed like that and she stared at him, fighting the temptation to take the one step that would close the space between them and put her back into his arms.

His eyes narrowed as they stared at each other. She realized how he looked at her and how she probably appeared to him. "That was sort of...dazzling. I better go now," she whispered.

"I know you don't intend to, but I think you might bring me back to life," he said, still looking intently at her. He placed his fingers on her chin, tilting her head as he gazed into her eyes. "One thing, Talia. I have to be truthful. I loved Regina and I don't think I can ever love again. I miss her every day that goes by. Remember, this is a proposal for a marriage of convenience, not love."

"I understand that you still love your wife even though she's gone and I can cope with that. I don't expect us to fall in love." She said those words, but her thoughts went in a different direction. She couldn't stop thinking about his kiss. A kiss that made her want to step right back into his embrace, wrap her arms around him and kiss him again. If one kiss could do this to her, she thought, how would she be after a night of raging hot sex? Could she keep from falling in love with him?

His voice broke through her thoughts. "What we just conjured up between us wasn't love."

No, it was a raging inferno because of the sexiest kiss ever.

"Oh, Nick," she said, her heart pounding and her voice raspy, "it may not be smart to do, but I need to give you one more kiss of thanks for giving me my dream." Stepping closer, she flung her arms around his neck, and standing on tiptoe, she kissed him, again pouring all her gratitude, excitement and happiness into another kiss.

Instantly, his arms circled her waist and he pulled her up hard against his body as he leaned over her and kissed her in return, his tongue moving over hers, stroking hers, setting her ablaze once more. She moaned with pleasure, felt his hard erection press against her. She finally broke away to gasp for breath.

They stared in silence at each other as if they were just seeing each other for the first time.

"I think I might be getting a bonus in this marriage on top of becoming Hattie's mom," she whispered.

"We both are," he said.

With a little shake, she tried to get back to the moment and glanced down at Hattie to find the little girl happily tearing up the magazines.

"Oh, my goodness," Talia said, rushing to stop her.

"Don't worry about it," Nick urged. "That's all recycle stuff now. I've read everything there I'm going to read."

"She can't tear up magazines. Next thing you know she'll be tearing pages out of her books." She knelt beside her on the floor and pried the pages out of her little hands.

"Hattie, no, no, no," Talia said, shaking her head, while speaking gently. "We don't rip these up. Let's look at the pictures. See? Here's a little white dog," she said, showing Hattie a magazine with a dog picture.

Hattie pointed at it. "Doggy," she said, stabbing the picture with a small finger. "Doggy."

"Let's put the picture away in the box now."

Obediently, Hattie picked up the magazine and deposited it in the box.

In minutes they had the area cleaned up. Talia sat on the floor beside Hattie and glanced at Nick to find him sitting close at hand and watching her.

"We should get to know each other a little better as well as start making plans," he said. "Come over for dinner tomorrow night and bring Hattie. I'll get Kirby, my cook, to check with you about what Hattie can eat."

"Don't bother your cook about Hattie. I can bring what little she eats. And I'll bring her sippy cup. I'll take care of her."

"That's okay now, but Kirby will have to learn what Hattie needs."

She nodded. "Also, I'll make a list of the furniture she needs and we can talk about—" She broke off to stare at him. "I can't believe we're discussing marriage, even when I know it's a marriage of convenience."

"Talia, you're very appealing. I don't understand why you aren't taken, why men aren't lined up to take you out."

She laughed. "Thanks, but I never have dated a lot. As a teacher and now with Hattie, I'm not around single men very much and I don't really want to go out and I'm sure men can sense that." When Nick didn't look convinced, she added, "Maybe you and I just have some kind of weird chemistry between us. I figured that kiss was the norm for you."

"Our kiss a few minutes ago the norm? Oh, no. Regina and I were friends and then we fell in love and that makes a difference. Love changes everything. You and I are strangers."

"Does this change your feelings about the marriage of convenience?"

"Change my mind? Oh, no," he said, smiling at her. "Far from it. After the kiss we just shared, I'm still on fire and I'm more for this marriage of convenience than I was before. I think it's a workable idea. I want my child to have a mother who loves her. And the bedroom side of it may turn out to be a giant plus."

She felt tingles from the look in his eyes and the husky sexy tone in his voice. "I have to admit, those kisses just now were a giant bonus for me, too. I'm ready for some fun in my life." She smiled at him. "Just keep in mind the purpose in getting married."

Holding on to the nearest furniture, Hattie began to toddle away from Talia, who stood and picked her up. Talia gathered her things and put her purse and the big bag over her shoulder while she held Hattie with her other arm. "Wave bye-bye to Daddy," she instructed Hattie.

Hattie waved her chubby little hand.

"Very good," Talia said and smiled at Hattie.

"It's going to take me a bit of time to get used to being Daddy," Nick said. "Even though I was one, Artie was too little to talk or know what was going on. I didn't get called Dada or anything. I'll have to get accustomed to my new status."

"That's fine. She won't know you're adjusting to it. Good night, Nick."

"You're not going to kiss me good-night?" he asked and she saw the twinkle in his eyes and realized he was teasing.

"I think we did that sufficiently for tonight. On the other hand, I think it would make her happier to know she has parents who are compatible," she said, smiling at him. Still holding Hattie with one arm, she placed her other hand on his shoulder and leaned close to kiss him on the cheek, feeling the short stubble.

His arm circled her waist and he kissed her briefly on the mouth and released her to smile at her. "She looks happy, so I suppose you're right."

Nick walked to the car with her, opening the car

door and watching while she fastened Hattie into the car seat.

Finally Talia was buckled in the driver's seat, ready to go, and Nick closed the door, leaning down to talk to her through the open window. "I'll send a car to pick you up for dinner tomorrow night. My butler has kids. He can go tomorrow with my chauffeur and they can get a car seat for Hattie and get it installed and then I'll send the limo for you. How's that?"

"It seems as if it would be easier for me to just drive to the ranch."

He shook his head. "If it's all right with you, I'll send the limo."

Startled, Talia nodded and realized life with Nick was going to be different from life as she had always known it. Limos, butlers, chauffeurs, trusts— her world was going to change drastically, thanks to Madeline and Hattie. It would change for the better because some things would be easier. She thought about Nick's kiss and felt hot all over, wanting his arms around her again. That was going to be a monumental difference. Would it work out without love between them? She didn't think he would get over his loss for a long time and she didn't expect him to fall in love.

Talia couldn't picture her life in the near future. She couldn't imagine going from teaching to living on a ranch. Besides taking care of her precious little Hattie, she would get to paint and draw, something she'd never had time to do. And then there'd be the nights with Nick, sitting around the dinner table, sharing private time once Hattie had gone down for the night. Then...

"Talia?" he prompted.

Coming out of her daze, she nodded at him. "Sorry, this is a monumental change that never occurred to me and I got lost in my thoughts. I'm not going to argue about you sending a limo for us," she said, smiling and shaking her head.

"Let's get married soon, Talia. Hattie is my daughter. Frankly, I'd feel better if she had a little more security in her life than you're able to provide."

"That's true, Nick, but sending a limo isn't keeping a low profile."

"I know, but it's safer. If we're going to marry, let's go ahead and do so. You can have a small wedding, can't you?"

"Oh, yes. It's my second wedding. I don't want another fancy formal white wedding dress this time. I don't have family. I have a few close friends I'd like to invite. You're the one with family and heaven knows how many friends," she answered, thinking she was marrying an incredibly handsome man. He had looked handsome and appealing to her before he proposed and kissed her, but now she was dazzled by him. Looking at his mouth, his full lower lip, she wanted to kiss him again.

"I've had one big wedding. I'm not having another, especially when it's a marriage of convenience," he said. "We'll have a very small wedding, maybe a slightly larger reception because my friends might as well meet Hattie and you. Is that okay with you?"

"Yes, whatever you want," she said. "And about the honeymoon… I'm so excited over Hattie and my future, I don't think one is necessary."

"That's fine with me. One more thing you might think about… Hattie's name. I want to change it. You'll be a Duncan soon and Madeline is gone and so is her family. You'll be able to see to it that Hattie knows Madeline was her blood mother, but I would like her to have the Duncan name."

"I think that's a good idea. I'll always make sure she knows about Madeline, but you're her dad. I think she should be Hattie Duncan."

"What about a middle name?"

"She doesn't have one. Madeline couldn't think of one and said she didn't need it anyway. You could give her Madeline for a middle name. Or Madeline's last name—Prentiss."

Nick thought for a moment, obviously trying out the names in his head. "Not Madeline," he decreed. "Some kids might call her Hattie Maddie. So let's go with Prentiss. Hattie Prentiss Duncan. Has a good ring to it."

"That's fine with me, Nick."

"Talia, this is going to be good. You'll be good for my little girl. She'll be loved and it will be almost a seamless transition for her. It's an enormous relief."

"I hope you grow to love her, Nick."

"I will. I'll do my best to be a good dad." He stepped back from the car. "I'll see you tomorrow night," he said. Wind caught locks of his brown hair, tangling them above his forehead. He smiled at her and just his smile made her pulse race. It would be so easy to fall in love with her handsome future husband. She would have to constantly remind herself to guard her heart, even though she didn't think it was going to be possible.

But right now, she wouldn't worry. She wouldn't let anything negatively impact this wonderful night. She would be Hattie's legal mother. She would be a stay-at-home mom to the little girl she loved. Hattie was so adorable, she was certain Nick too would love his little girl just as he had loved his son. They'd have an amazing life together, the three of them. How could they not? Nick had fulfilled her deepest wish.

She thought about their kisses and her heart pounded, desire making her wish his arms were around her and his mouth on hers again. The man could kiss like no other she had known. He was the sexiest man she had ever met. Put that together with Nick giving her the deepest desire of her heart and he became the most appealing male on the globe.

She couldn't stop thinking about him as she drove back to her place. His kisses made her hot just thinking about them. What would it be like to make love? She tingled all over, and before she combusted, she told herself to wrangle her sexy thoughts and concentrate on her driving.

Easier said than done.

That night, long after she was in bed and Hattie was asleep, Talia lay awake, staring into the darkness, still remembering being in Nick's arms and kissing him. He had clearly warned her he would not fall in love. She needed to take sex the way Nick would—without getting emotionally involved.

"I can't do that," she whispered aloud in the dark bedroom. She knew if she was intimate with Nick, gave him her body, her heart would go along with it. She was going to love him for giving her Hattie. She could try to keep a wall around her heart, but Nick was too appealing, too sexy, and he had given her the one thing in this world she wanted most.

She had to go into this marriage of convenience knowing that was all it was to Nick. A convenience. He had given her Hattie, and as long as he gave Hattie the love of a father for his child, Talia knew she shouldn't expect anything more.

She adjusted her pillow and turned on her side, but sleep was elusive. A half hour later, still wide-awake, she went to check on Hattie.

She stood beside her crib, watching Hattie sleep. "You'll have a daddy now," she whispered, looking at Hattie curled on her side, the pink bunny held tightly in the crook of her arm. "You'll have a daddy, a chauffeur and heaven knows who else—and you're going to take me into that world with you." Relief and joy filled her. At the same time, doubt pecked at her thoughts. Would she be able to adjust and get along with Nick? Keep Nick happy? She couldn't answer those questions. She was marrying a man who was a stranger.

"I'm going to marry your daddy and be your mommy forever," she said softly, focusing instead on the joy that welled up again in her heart. "Sweet baby, I get to be your mommy. I will love you all my life and take care of you the best I can. And your daddy? I'll just have to learn to live with your daddy, who doesn't love me. As long as he loves you—and he will—we'll be fine. As long as he kisses the way he did tonight, it should be a blast being married to him. He has to be the sexiest man on this earth. I'm going to try to keep my heart intact, but with kisses like tonight's, I don't think I can. Nick Duncan. Mrs. Nicholas Duncan with daughter Hattie Prentiss Duncan." The names sounded good on her lips.

"It seems impossible, doesn't it?" she asked the sleeping baby. "Only it is possible and it's going to happen. I'm going to marry Nick Duncan. He doesn't love me and he never will, but he's giving me my fantasy. Is he going to break my heart?" She shrugged. "Nothing would ever hurt like losing you, Hattie, and now you'll be my baby forever. And I will try to be the best mother possible. I will love you with all my heart."

She kissed the top of Hattie's head and slipped out before she stirred. As she moved through her small house, she felt dazed. Her life had changed in the past few hours, a change she hadn't expected. In a short while she would be marrying Nick Duncan and have a sprawling ranch and an elegant mansion to call home. Not to mention the sexiest man ever beside her.

But she knew their marriage would never involve love. Time might carry him away from the pain and loss he had suffered, but she didn't expect him to fall in love with her.

Talia knew loss, too. She had been hurt badly in her first marriage. She had lost her mother and her dad. She had suffered two miscarriages. Having endured all that, she knew they understood each other's pain.

Again, she smiled as she thought about the joyous, happy fact that she wouldn't lose Hattie. For that she would be forever grateful to Nick and she would do her best to help him be a daddy to Hattie. That was the best with Nick she could hope for and that had to be enough.

She returned to her bed, but knowing she was too wide-awake to sleep, she pulled a pen and paper from her nightstand and set about making her lists. One for the baby furniture and items she'd need to purchase, and another of the few people she'd like to invite to the wedding. Nick's guest list would no doubt be more plentiful, with his business contacts, friends and family.

What would his family think about her? The

thought struck her out of the blue. And what would they think about Nick marrying to give Hattie a mother? His brothers and grandmother would know he wasn't in love. Would his family accept her?

More important, would they accept Hattie—a little girl whom Nick had known nothing about?

Doubt started creeping in, quietly but steadily, and by the time Talia shut off her light, she knew she'd lie awake till morning.

What was she thinking, marrying a man she barely knew with a family she didn't know? Marrying a man she didn't love and who didn't—wouldn't—love her? How could they make this marriage of convenience work?

Four

Nick went up the walk to his grandmother's house, which was the original ranch house and much smaller than his home or Stan's palatial ranch house. His gaze ran over the house that was smaller than his. The original part was built pre–Civil War. Each Duncan to live in it added to the house and made changes. It had been repaired, improved and enlarged through the years, and Nick liked the old place, but he wouldn't live in it. He climbed the wooden steps to the porch, walked to the front door and rang the bell as he entered so they would know he was coming.

"Hello, Mr. Nick," Braden said as he walked toward the front door as Nick stepped inside.

"Hi, Braden," Nick said, greeting the man who

served as cook and butler for Nick's grandmother. Braden Aldridge had worked for them since Nick was a kid. He wore his usual white shirt and black trousers and black boots.

A woman came down the hall and Nick smiled as he greeted the former nurse and now a companion for his grandmother. Her round face was framed by brown hair streaked with gray in a pixie cut. "Hi, Ida. The weather's good. I thought maybe Grandmother would be outside."

"She likes the air-conditioning a bit better," Ida said. "As always, she's looking forward to your visit."

"Something smells good, Braden."

"A pot roast. I'm sure you'll be asked to stay to eat with her."

"I can't today, but I hope I can get some to take with me. No one can beat your pot roast."

"She supervises. It's sort of 'our' pot roast."

"Grandmother has always been a good cook. We'll see if I get an invitation. Whether I do or I don't, I'll come by the kitchen before I leave anyway," Nick said, smiling at the cook, who was one of the best.

"How's she feeling?" he asked Ida as he walked beside her.

"She's fine and happy you're coming to see her."

"Good. I have some family news that she can tell you. I hope it doesn't upset her."

"Uh-oh. I was going to say that I can't wait to hear the news...unless it's bad news."

"No. Whatever she tells you, I think it's good news, and I think I'm doing what's best, but it'll give her a shock."

"Now I am curious," Ida said, smiling at him. "She's in the back and anxious to see you. Maybe I'll see you at dinner."

"Well, not tonight. I have company." He left her and walked down the hall to enter a large sunroom with a view of the patio to the south.

"Hello," he said, entering the room and crossing to his grandmother, who sat in her favorite recliner with her feet propped up. Switching off the television, she sat up as he leaned down to kiss her powdered cheek, getting a whiff of her usual lilac perfume. "You look comfortable," he said.

"I'm very comfortable. Now, this is not the usual time you come by for a visit, so what's up?"

He sat across from her, thinking how little she had changed over the years. Her gray hair was in its usual bun at the back of her head. She was tall and thin, but stronger than she looked. Her eyes were light brown, unlike his or his brothers'. Her glasses had slipped down her nose and she removed them, rubbing her eyes and looking at him.

"So what brings you visiting?" she asked. "You can't possibly smell that pot roast from your house, but I know it's one of your favorites."

"That it is," he said, wondering how she was

going to take his news. He hoped they didn't have conflict over his marriage or over Hattie. "No, I didn't come calling because of the pot roast."

"Well, you might as well stay and eat some because I know how you like it and we have a lot."

"Thank you, but I can't stay because I'm having company and I'm going back to Dallas this afternoon."

"I'll send some home with you."

"I'd like that." They sat looking at each other and he knew he might as well tell her his news and get her reaction over with and go from there. He leaned forward, placing his arms on his knees and looking into her brown eyes. "I'm going to tell you two things that I think will shock you, so I'm just giving you warning now."

"Am I going to faint?"

He smiled. "I don't think so. You never have so far."

Her eyes twinkled and he wondered if she could take his next announcement as calmly. "Horace called and said a woman named Talia Barton wanted to see me and I should see her."

"Horace? Our attorney, Horace?"

"That's right. Here's why. A couple of years ago I was at a party and had an evening with a beautiful woman, Madeline Prentiss, who had a rising career in the music world. Talia Barton was her teacher and her friend. Fourteen months ago, this woman, Madeline Prentiss, gave birth to my daughter."

"Oh, my heavens, Nick. I'm a great-grandmother to a little girl?"

"Yes. Madeline didn't have family and Talia helped her care for the baby while Madeline pursued a singing career."

"Why didn't the mother tell you about the baby? Do you think it is actually yours?"

"She is definitely mine. I had a DNA test done. Talia Barton told me that Madeline thought I was still so in love with Regina and so torn over losing her and Artie that I wouldn't want to hear about the baby. Several months ago Madeline died in a car wreck. Talia has taken care of little Hattie and she's like a mother to Hattie. Now the state wants to take Hattie because Talia has no legal papers to show that Madeline wanted her to have Hattie."

"This baby is a Duncan. Your baby. You can't let the state take your baby. This woman came to tell you so the state won't get your baby?"

"That's correct. She wants me to be a dad to my daughter even though it means she will have to give up Hattie, a little girl she loves like her own. Talia will have to give up Hattie to the state or to me. She preferred me to take her. With Madeline gone, Talia is mama to Hattie." He took a deep breath and waited.

"You have a little girl," Myra said. "I am a great-grandmother to a little girl. How old is she?"

"Fourteen months," he repeated patiently, giving her time to absorb the first part of his news.

"Have you seen her?"

"Yes. She looks like the Duncans."

"Oh, my. You really think so? So you're going to raise a little girl. My goodness. I'm in shock, Nick."

"Grandmother, there's more. Talia Barton has been a mother to Hattie in every way except by blood and by law. She loves my daughter and takes good care of her." He swallowed hard. "I've proposed to Talia. She knows I'm not in love with her, but it is a way she can keep Hattie and Hattie will have the mama she loves."

"Nick, have you lost your senses? You can't marry a stranger because she knows how to take care of a baby. Mercy sakes. Don't tie your life up with some woman you don't know."

"I've already proposed. Hattie will have a mother who loves her."

"Nick, what is the matter with you?" she said, her voice getting louder. "You don't know this woman at all."

"I know Talia a little. She's an art teacher in a two-year college. That means the school system has checked her out to a certain extent. More important, I know she adores my daughter. She contacted me instead of letting the state just take Hattie away. If it weren't for Talia, I wouldn't even know I have a daughter."

"You know nothing about this woman except what you just told me and she knows nothing about you."

"She does know something about me. She had me checked out by a PI."

"She checked you out?" his grandmother shrieked. Nick merely nodded.

"Nick, our family is known by all Texans. We've been here since the battle at the Alamo."

He tried to hang on to his patience because he had expected her to react exactly the way she was. "Grandmother, not all Texans know who we are. Talia wanted to make sure I would be safe to leave Hattie with because if I didn't check out, she would have let the state take her."

"Oh, my word," she said, frowning and rubbing her hands together. "Don't be so foolish. Marrying a total stranger—that's asking for all sorts of trouble."

"I've invited Talia for dinner. I want you and my brothers to meet her and then you can tell me what you think. You'll meet Hattie, too.

"Talia is very nice. She's intelligent and she'll make a good mother. And now you have a little girl in the family," he said.

"A little child will adjust to someone else who is kind to her. Someone like you. We all will be good to her. She'll have a family and you do not need to marry a woman you just met. Don't get your life all tangled up. You know you won't be happy with her after Regina and little Arthur. Don't marry this Talia person."

"I think you'll like Talia."

"I can't imagine why you think that. And you don't know anything about little girls."

Nick ignored his grandmother's statement. He knew this would be difficult, so he simply forged ahead with his plan. "I'd like to have a family dinner Friday night. How's that? I'll send the limo to get you. We'll have dinner here on the ranch."

"Nick, oh, I'm so glad you have a little girl. What a joy she's going to be," she said, talking more to herself than to him. "We can take care of her. But you don't need to marry this woman. I do wish you hadn't committed yourself. Get out of it."

"Hold your opinion until after you meet her. See if you like her. I've got to run now. I'm going back to Dallas and I'll have Talia and Hattie for dinner tonight."

"You're not listening to me. Please don't do this in haste and regret it for years."

He brushed a kiss on her cheek. "I love you, Grandmother, and I know you want what's best for me. I know you'll love Hattie and I think you'll like Talia."

His grandmother shook her head. "Nick, I'll worry every day about you if you marry this woman."

He laughed. "Worrywart Grandmother is what you are. I know it's because you love me. You'll meet them Friday."

With that, he blew her a kiss and left her. His thoughts jumped ahead to tonight and seeing Talia again. In a lot of ways he was glad Talia had accepted his proposal for a marriage of convenience. She loved Hattie too much to miss this chance to become her legal mother forever. He also had mixed feelings and a streak of guilt because he still loved Regina and missed her and he missed little Artie. He knew he would probably grow to love Hattie, too, but right now there were so many hurtful memories. Longing swamped him for his wife and baby and he knew no one would ever take their place.

He stopped by the kitchen, and before he could say anything, Braden held out a covered container. "Here's your pot roast."

Nick smiled. "Thanks, Braden. This is a super treat. The smell is killing me. I can't wait to sink my teeth into this. You're the best."

"Well, Miss Myra steps in here to stir every few hours."

Nick laughed. "I'll bet she does. And I bet she does a lot of taste testing."

Braden smiled. "Yes, she does."

"Thanks again," Nick said and left, forgetting the pot roast when he reached the car and thinking about his grandmother's warnings.

He was Hattie's father, so he would claim her and raise her, and it seemed the best solution to him to get Talia's help and keep her with Hattie.

He loved his grandmother, but this time she was worrying for nothing.

* * *

Late that afternoon as he worked in his Dallas office, Nick heard his phone buzz with a text. He looked at it and saw Talia had to cancel their dinner appointment because she needed to meet with two parents over a problem their son had at school. She hadn't found a sitter yet and it seemed best to cancel dinner.

He sent her a text to come eat pot roast before meeting with the parents and leave Hattie with him. Talia replied that it would be easier to grab a bite before she went and let him feed Hattie. She would bring everything for Hattie.

Nick remembered kissing her—something he thought about at least once every sixty minutes all his waking hours. He could get aroused just remembering holding and kissing her. Her kisses consumed him and made him want to carry her off to bed and forget the world. This marriage was going to be more than he had expected. He'd proposed knowing he wanted a loving mother for Hattie. Now he knew he was getting a woman whose kisses promised the hottest sex he had ever experienced. He wanted this marriage soon. He wanted her in his bed as a way to erase the hurt and loneliness he had lived with for too long now.

He'd looked forward to spending the evening with Talia. But now he would be taking care of Hattie all by himself. Nick rubbed his neck. He should be able to feed Hattie, but he didn't have a high chair for her yet.

Leaving his Dallas office, Nick went home, called his attorney and set up the trusts for Talia and for Hattie. When it was time for their arrival, he went outside to wait for them. As he paced, he was assailed by memories of times he'd spent waiting for Regina and Artie to come home from shopping or a doctor appointment. Would he ever stop longing for his beloved wife and son?

Even more worrisome, was he rushing headlong into a marriage that would be a giant mistake as his grandmother predicted?

Talia parked and got Hattie out of the car seat. Nick came bounding to the car, his long legs covering the distance quickly. Her heartbeat quickened when she saw him. In jeans, boots and a black short-sleeved knit shirt, he looked purposeful, seemingly filled with energy, sexy and appealing, and she wished she could spend the evening with him.

When Nick took Hattie from Talia, their hands brushed, and she had the same intense awareness of touching him as before, bringing back instant memories of his kiss. She looked up at him, and when their gazes met, it was as if they'd made a sexual contact.

He turned to look at Hattie and smiled. "Hi, Hattie."

"Ho," she said, smiling at him.

"That's her 'hello.'" Talia stood by him and patted his arm, feeling the solid muscle.

"I'm sorry, but this afternoon was hectic and I was late getting her and getting home. I would have fed her, but I was afraid that would make me late for my appointment."

"That's fine. Feeding her shouldn't be difficult."

"I brought a chair for her. It's in the trunk of the car. If you'll get it, I'll take Hattie."

"Sure, I'll get it. Don't worry about us because we'll get along just fine," he said.

"You can heat the chopped carrots for her and give her some milk. I brought her little sippy cup and lid. She loves strawberries and I've cut up some small bites. It's all in this bag plus some of her toys. I'm sorry, but I need to run. Phone me if you have a question."

He caught her arm and held it. "Talia, I'll take good care of her. Don't worry about her." They looked at each other intently and she got lost in his gaze, acutely aware that his hand still lightly held her arm. Her attention shifted to his mouth and then she remembered what he had said.

"I'm sure you'll be great with her," she stated, her voice sounding slightly hoarse. How could he cause such an intense reaction just by casually touching her or looking at her? She didn't think he was paying any more attention to their conversation than she was. All she could think about was kissing him. Was she going to fall in love with him if she was around him often? If they married and had sex, would she be able to avoid a broken heart? The question was becoming more important because her reactions to him were intensifying.

"I've got to run," she said, looking at him and still mesmerized by the way he gazed at her. She knew his thoughts were on their kiss, too, especially when his eyes lowered to her mouth.

With an effort she turned away and slipped behind the steering wheel. "I'll see you in a couple of hours. Call if you have a question or have difficulty."

"Sure. Don't worry. We won't have difficulty," he said, smiling at Hattie as she ran her fingers over his jaw. "She likes my whiskers."

"She's fascinated by you. You're the first man in her life and this is discovery for her. You'll be a good dad, Nick."

He smiled at Hattie. "I'm glad you have confidence in me. I hope it's contagious. I usually feel on top of challenges, but this one throws me. I don't know anything about baby girls. Do you care, Hattie?" he asked and she giggled while she still ran her fingers over his chin.

"I'm glad my face entertains her," he said.

"I'm going to be late," Talia said, more to herself than to Nick. "You might want to distract her so she doesn't see me leave. She's getting so she doesn't want me to leave her. I brought some toys in the bag, and if you'll take her inside and get them out, she'll forget about me."

She watched as Nick turned toward the house, talking to Hattie as he went. Then she drove away.

She tried to concentrate on the road, but it was impossible to avoid thinking about Nick. Since her disastrous marriage, she hadn't wanted to fall in love again with any man. And now she certainly didn't want to fall in love with Nick. It was obvious his heart was locked away. Sure, they had some hot chemistry between them, but that wasn't the bedrock of a solid marriage. Love was. And Nick was still in love with his late wife.

How many times would she have to remind herself of that?

As she turned at the green light, she forced her thoughts down a different path. Instead of worrying about guarding her heart against Nick, she reveled in the fact that Hattie would legally be her baby. She couldn't weigh the pros and cons of this convenient marriage. There was just one giant consideration—Hattie. Along with being her mother came the fun of going to bed with Nick.

Talia hoped this appointment didn't take too long because she wanted to get back to Nick and Hattie. Despite his reassuring words, he seemed nervous with the prospect of taking care of his daughter alone. Smiling, Talia shook her head. What was she thinking? Nick had been a dad. He was intelligent, capable, dealt with all sorts of situations and animals on that ranch. He would be fine with Hattie and Hattie would probably like being with Nick. How could he not cope with a little fourteen-month-old toddler?

"Darlin', here's a little bag all packed just for you. Let's see what's in it," Nick said, sitting on the floor in front of Hattie. He opened the bag and reached in to pull out a small white teddy bear. "Look, Hattie, here's your bear."

"Mine. Bear," she repeated, snatching it out of his hand and hugging it.

She tossed it aside and reached into the bag to pull out a small soft ball, which she threw across the room then turned to get the next toy. Nick held the bag and watched her, marveling that this was his child. He was still in shock from discovering this little girl who was going to become a major part of his life. Hattie pulled out another brightly colored box with a handle. When she turned the handle, it played a tune and she worked at turning the crank, her tiny fingers clinging to the small handle. "I should have known about you, little darlin', from the time you were born. I'm glad you're in my life now. I have a lot to learn about you."

She pulled out another toy and tossed it aside, reaching in to get another. Toys flew in various directions and he let her do what she wanted. She reached deep into the bag, pulled out a book and handed it to him.

"You want me to read *Peter Rabbit* to you? Come here, sweetie, and we'll read the book." Standing, he picked up her and her book and went to the rocker to sit and hold her, remembering holding Artie, who'd been so tiny compared to Hattie.

"Here's another bunny," he said, pointing to the rabbit on the cover.

"Bun," she said, sitting up and looking around. She got off his lap and held his knee as she reached for a chair. "Bun," she said again, more insistently as she clung to the chair and took a wobbly step, grabbing a table. She stretched out her arm and opened and closed her hand, and he spotted the pink bunny on the floor. He crossed the room to retrieve it, handing it to her.

"Here's your bunny. What you want, I think," he said, picking her up again as she hugged the bunny. Then she pointed to the chair.

"You seem to know what you want. We'll read about this bunny." He rocked her as he read. He hoped he could be a good dad. If he could rely on Talia, he thought they would get along fine.

After he read the book, he thought about Talia, who was bringing him back into the world. Her hot kisses ignited lust and thoughts of seduction. She was going to complicate his life more than it already had been. The minute they made love, emotions would come to life as well as physical desire, and right now he was struggling to get over mourning his losses and coping with the knowledge that he was the daddy of a little girl. A little girl who was pointing her finger at the book he held.

"Bun," she repeated.

He figured she wanted him to read the book again. "I'm guessing Talia reads to you a lot. Okay," he said, opening the cover. "Let's see about Peter Rabbit again."

It was almost 9:00 p.m. when Nick stood, carrying Hattie in his arms as he went to the door and opened it to greet Talia.

"I'm sorry I'm late," she said. She looked down at Hattie, curled against him as she slept. "How did she get along?" Talia asked.

"Don't ask about her. Ask if I survived. She was fine as long as I didn't get out of her sight and gave her one hundred percent of my attention. She's got the energy of the whole front line of a pro football team. For a little person who can barely toddle around, she's busy, and this house isn't set up for a baby. We may be babyproof in the family room now because she's thrown everything she could get her hands on if I didn't move it first. She's been asleep about five minutes—" He paused and his eyes narrowed. "You're laughing at me."

"I'm smiling because I'm glad you two have had a fun evening. I think you'll be a success as a dad," she said. "You'll get the kinks worked out and get the hang of having her in your house and in your life. It just takes a little time."

"I know you're laughing at me. I just couldn't

keep up with her and there must be some trick to getting food down her instead of all over both of us. She wasn't thrilled with the carrots."

"Usually she likes carrots. I tried to bring what she really likes. She might not have been very hungry. Looks as if you have a bit of her dinner on you," she said, brushing tiny orange bits off his jaw. He was aware of her fingers touching him. She smelled wonderful with some exotic perfume and she looked gorgeous in a red dress with a straight skirt that clung to curves that made him forget the problems of the evening.

"Would my son have been like this? He seemed peaceful and easy except in the middle of the night when one of us had to walk with him. He didn't sleep too well through the night."

"Nick, he was two months old. That's a tiny baby. He couldn't toddle or crawl around the house. You would have gotten used to taking care of him. You'll get accustomed to Hattie. You're just starting," she said, taking out her handkerchief and wiping carrots off his shirt. "This will all come out in the laundry."

He caught another whiff of her perfume and was aware how close she stood, conscious of each brush of her fingers on his jaw. He wanted to put Hattie down and wrap Talia in his embrace.

"You really are laughing at me."

She looked up at him with twinkling blue eyes. "No, I'm not," she said as she smiled at him. "I'm happy all went well between the two of you." She glanced around the room that now had baby crackers scattered on the furniture and the floor. "You did a good job, but I can take her home now."

"Oh, no, you don't go now. I want some adult conversation. We still have some time. You sit with me and we'll talk. Want a glass of wine, a beer, pop, anything?"

"Sure. Sit and I'll get it. What would you like?"

"I'll wait. I have my hands full at the moment."

While Nick rocked Hattie, he watched Talia go to the bar and get a glass of ice water. She turned off all but one small lamp before she walked back to him. Nick watched Talia's every move, looking at her legs when she sat opposite him and crossed them. He wondered how soft they'd be if he ever got to touch them. The only sound in the room was the faint, rhythmic creak of the rocker. The one light brought out the highlights in Talia's long, silky-looking hair. Her thickly lashed eyes looked larger than ever. When his gaze lowered to her full red lips, he thought about their kiss. She was such a beautiful woman and again he wondered why no man had claimed her. She deserved the love of a great guy who'd cherish her. He realized that she would get cheated by agreeing to a loveless marriage of convenience. He drew a deep breath, reminding himself that she was getting what she desperately wanted, just as he would get what he wanted from their marriage agreement.

"Talia, spread her little blanket on the floor and let me put her on it to sleep."

"Sure." He watched her skirt pull tightly, revealing a sexy ass. A slight slit in the skirt revealed more of her long, gorgeous legs as she knelt and spread the baby blanket.

He knelt beside her, placing Hattie on the blanket. Still sleeping and holding her bunny close, she turned on her side.

He walked over to take Talia's hand and pull her to her feet. "Just a kiss. You look luscious and I want you in my arms for a kiss."

His heartbeat raced and he was already hot thinking about her and watching her move around. He wanted her, and when her gaze went to his mouth, his heart pounded. He slipped his arm around her tiny waist, pulling her against him as he leaned down to kiss her, brushing her velvety lips first with his and then coaxing her mouth open as he deepened the kiss. She was soft, enticing and sexy, and he wanted to hold and kiss her the rest of the night. He knew she wouldn't let that happen, but he was desperate for even one kiss. He brushed her mouth with his again. Her eyes were closed, her fingers on the back of his neck, and she was pressed tightly against him. As he gazed at her, she opened her eyes to look up at him.

"You've brought me back to life," he whispered, running one hand lightly over her breast. "I want you. I want you naked in my arms all night. I want to kiss you all over. Let's get on with this wedding so you can move in with me."

"That's fine with me," she whispered.

"Give me a date. How soon can we have the wedding?"

Five

How could she think? With Nick showering light kisses on her ear and throat, she tingled from head to toe. Conscious thought was a distant memory, especially when his hands trailed down her back, over her derriere, pulling her up against him so that she could feel his arousal.

"When, Talia?" he whispered against her neck.

His prompt seemed to rouse her from her sensual stupor and she pulled back to look at him. She ignored the flare of gold in his green eyes and forced herself to focus instead on a mental calendar.

"How about the first Saturday in June? That way, school is out and I'll be through."

"That date is fine with me," he said in a raspy

voice. He caught her chin with his fingers and gazed down at her.

"I want you, Talia. You're bringing me back to life."

"You're giving me my heart's desire, my fantasy dream, so I'm glad I'm doing something for you," she whispered, showering light kisses on his lips, the corner of his mouth, his throat.

"Stay here tonight," he whispered.

"I can't. I have school tomorrow and you don't own a crib. This is not the night. Wait for the wedding and then we'll have furniture—"

Her words stopped when his mouth covered hers and his arms tightened around her, drawing her against him. When his tongue slid past her lips and she opened to him in return, she forgot whatever she was about to say. She could only revel in the feel of him. His tongue stroked hers, stirring hot desire. His hard erection pressed against her, inviting her to thrust her hips against him.

Somehow she managed to pull away, and she opened her eyes to look up at him. He was breathing as hard as she was, and his eyes had darkened to a rich emerald green.

"Nick, I'll try my best to make all this work for the three of us," she managed to say. "This is going to be wonderful for Hattie."

"I agree. I want you to meet my family, so we'll plan dinner at the ranch. I can send the limo to pick you and Hattie up and you plan to stay the night. How's this Friday if I can round up my brothers?"

Any day was good for her. Right now all she wanted was to spend a night in his bed.

"Friday is fine," she said.

"Can you pick out a crib after school tomorrow? Call me when you find it and I'll buy it and I'll see to it that it's delivered and set up by Friday. Don't you worry about those arrangements at all. I can take care of that."

"Gladly. You're accustomed to getting things done the way you want them, aren't you?"

"A lot of things," he replied, "but I couldn't do one damn thing about Regina and Artie."

She expected to see sadness enter his eyes, as it usually did when he spoke of the family he'd lost. The flow of passion ebbed in their green depths, replaced by a wave of serious intent. But at least it wasn't sadness.

"Talia, I need to warn you. The first time you meet Grandmother, she'll be a grump because she doesn't want me to marry when I don't know you. But I think she's going to like having a great-granddaughter."

"I hope so. I love Hattie so much, I want everyone else to love her, too. Particularly the people in her family, all of you who are blood relatives. I'm the one who isn't."

"I'm sure they'll come round," he told her.

"It's getting late, Nick. I'd better take Hattie and go."

He shook his head. "Stay awhile and let's make some plans."

She couldn't say no to him, so she sat beside him in one of the two upholstered wing chairs that were close together and near Hattie.

He leaned over and took her hand. "You know, when I lost Artie, I got rid of his furniture. I just closed the door on the room and never went back in. You have free rein as far as the new furniture goes, and the decor. In fact, please do change it. I want the room to be Hattie's now. How fast can you get that done?"

"I can look at the room Friday night when we're on the ranch. Saturday, if I get right back to Dallas, I can pick out the furniture and make arrangements to have it delivered. I think I can get that much done very soon."

"Excellent," he said.

"I want it as soon as possible, too," she said, knowing the minute she became Mrs. Nick Duncan, she would become Hattie's stepmother. "If we have to, we can marry and have a crib or cradle in my bedroom while we get the nursery finished. Nick, as soon as we marry, I want to start the adoption process. I will always tell her about her mother, but I want everything tied up legally so she's my child."

"That suits me. So does having the wedding as soon as possible. The sooner we marry, the better. My attorney will deal with the state agency."

Talia looked at the child sleeping peacefully on

the blanket and felt a rush of love. She had to be doing the right thing for Hattie. Nick would grow to love Hattie, she was sure. So would his family. But would they accept her—someone Nick was bringing into his family when he didn't love her and he barely knew her. How many of them had tried to talk him out of marrying her? What kind of future would she have with this marriage bargain?

Late Friday afternoon Nick sent a limo to Dallas to get Talia and Hattie. The chauffeur, Dusty Jones, carried their bags, and then with Hattie buckled into her new child seat in the limo, they left for the ranch.

As they slowed and stopped in front, Talia's gaze swept over the sprawling house that would soon be home for Hattie and her. Made of wood and stone, it was far less formal than the palatial mansion that was Nick's Dallas home. But would she ever grow accustomed to it as her home?

Nick sat on the porch, and as the limo approached the house, he stood and walked to the top of the steps. Her pulse took the usual jump at the sight of him. In a long-sleeved blue Western-style shirt, jeans and boots, he kept her pulse racing. He didn't wear a hat and his light brown hair was blowing slightly with the breeze. Dusty stopped and came back to open the door for her, but Nick got there first. He reached out to take Hattie from her, his hands brushing hers. The instant they made the slight contact, her insides fluttered.

"Here's Daddy," she said as Nick held Hattie easily and reached out his hand to help Talia get out.

Hattie looked up at him. "Dada," she said, touching his jaw.

"I told you my face fascinates her," he said, smiling at Hattie, who smiled in return.

"Dada."

"That's right, sweet baby girl." He turned to Talia. "Come in. I'll take you to your suite. The new crib is set up, new sheets are washed and on your bed, and it's ready for you and Hattie."

"That's great, Nick. I'm anxious to meet your family and jittery, too."

"You meet—what? More than a hundred new students at the start of each semester? And I'll bet you're not jittery about them. My brothers are looking forward to meeting you. My grandmother is, too, even if she won't admit it. And they're all excited to meet Hattie."

"Meeting students at the start of the school year is entirely different. They have to accept me as their teacher and we're not going to live together. This is a relationship that's for better or for worse, one that'll have an effect on the rest of all our lives. Of course I'm jittery. Your grandmother sounds a little formidable because it's obvious she doesn't want me in the family."

"I do. End of argument. Grandmother will adjust." He led her into the house and up the wide staircase to the second floor. "And just wait until she meets Hattie. I know my grandmother and she's going to love Hattie. You'll get the fallout from that, so stop worrying. And my brothers?" he tossed over his shoulder at her. "Those guys will think you're wonderful."

She laughed. "I hope you're right."

He stopped in front of a door at the top of the stairs. "Here's your suite. Mine is next to it, right there," he said, pointing to the right. "And Hattie's nursery is next to it on the other side. In fact, the two rooms have a connecting door inside."

When he opened a door, she glimpsed Hattie's adjoining suite that was devoid of furniture with bare wood flooring. Her living area was spacious, filled with inviting, comfortable furnishings in primary colors. A sofa was upholstered in material with red and blue poppies against a white background, and there were red throw pillows. Dark blue wing chairs were on either side of the sofa and a circular glass table was in front of it.

"This is so pretty, Nick."

"You can change it if you want," he said. "I had a decorator change it last year," he added and she heard the harsh note in his voice. She also noticed that he didn't take her into the adjoining nursery. Instead, he turned to the opposite direction.

"There's your bedroom," he said, leading her into the space.

She moved ahead of him into another large room with a king-size bed covered in a comforter done in the same poppy motif. Near the bed stood a new white crib.

"This is wonderful, Nick. I think my whole house would easily fit into this suite and have room left over."

She ushered him to the door, knowing how difficult it must be for him to be near the nursery. Wanting to give him the out he no doubt desired, she said, "I need some time to get Hattie changed and get myself ready before your family arrives. So shoo." She smiled at him and couldn't help but notice how relieved he looked when he shut the door behind him.

Shortly before six Talia checked herself in a mirror again. She wore a conservative aqua dress with a scoop neckline, short sleeves and a straight skirt. Her hair fell in spiral curls that framed her face. She wore matching high heels and a silver bracelet, silver hoop earrings and a silver necklace. She felt jittery, an uncustomary nervousness, because she was uncertain about the evening. She hoped she could please Nick's grandmother and she certainly wanted all his family to love Hattie. She turned to survey Hattie again.

Wearing a pink dress with pink bows in her hair, Hattie sat on the floor, happily playing with a big clear plastic ball filled with plastic butterflies.

Talia heard Nick's boots on the oak floor of the hallway and her heart skipped a beat as he entered the room. He wore a white dress shirt, a silver-and-turquoise bolo tie, charcoal slacks and his black boots.

"Look. Here's your daddy," she said cheerfully as she walked to meet Nick, wrapping her arms around him to hug him. "Hello, Daddy," she said, looking at Nick, knowing he was absolutely the most handsome man she had ever known. Definitely the sexiest.

"Well, hello, darlin'. The day just got better," he said, smiling at her and slipping his arms around her waist.

"I want her to learn to hug and be friendly with family," she said.

"I'm all for that," he said, squeezing her closer. He looked at her lips and she stepped away quickly, picking up Hattie before he could kiss her. She needed her wits about her tonight.

"Here's Daddy," she said, placing her hand on Nick's shoulder.

"Dada," Hattie said, smiling at him, and he took her from Talia.

"You look gorgeous," he told Talia, his gaze sweeping over her.

"Thank you," she said and smiled. "I'll admit that I'm nervous. I want them to like me."

"Stop worrying about my grandmother. As far as my brothers are concerned, they're going to love having you in the family and they'll all think you're gorgeous."

"I hope you're right about them. What about your grandmother's companion?"

"Ida Corwin? She's so quiet, you'll barely know she's here and usually she steps out of family events. She'll hang around with everyone after dinner to keep an eye on my grandmother."

He carried Hattie downstairs in one arm, while he held Talia's hand. She barely had time to get herself settled when his brothers arrived. Immediately, Talia saw the family resemblance. She met Stan, who was shorter than Nick and stockier. Adam, who looked the most like his oldest brother, and Blake, the only one with dark brown hair instead of lighter brown like the others. But they all had those Duncan signature green eyes flecked with gold.

When Nick tugged on her arm, Talia turned to face a tall, gray-haired woman. Nick introduced his grandmother, Myra Pierce. The woman didn't smile. She merely gave Talia a frosty greeting as she moved past her and sat in a wingback chair. Nick turned to a shorter woman, younger than his grandmother with friendly brown eyes and short hair streaked with gray. "This is Ida Corwin. Ida, I'd like you to meet Talia Barton.

"And here is the reason we're all together to-night," he said, picking up Hattie. "Grandmother, this is Hattie Prentiss. Of course, we'll have her name changed to Hattie Duncan as soon as we can process the paperwork." He held the baby toward

Myra. "You've had a great-grandson. Hattie is your first great-granddaughter."

"This is my great-granddaughter," Myra repeated, sounding surprised as she gazed at Hattie. "She's a beautiful little girl. She looks like all the Duncans, too."

"I think so," Talia said as Nick handed Hattie to Talia.

"I'll talk to my brothers while you get Grandmother acquainted with Hattie," Nick said and left them before anyone could protest.

"I'll go speak to the others," Ida said and left them also.

Myra glanced at Talia. "You're very happy to marry Nick," Myra said in a cold voice.

"Yes. Marriage to Nick makes me Hattie's mother," she said, smiling at the baby.

Stan appeared at Talia's side. "I want to join this conversation, and actually, I'm supposed to tell you that Nick wants to show you something. Do you think Hattie will let me hold her?"

"I think she'd be delighted," Talia said, handing Hattie to Stan. "Hattie, meet your soon-to-be uncle Stan." She turned to Myra. "If you'll excuse me, I'll see what Nick wants and be back."

She left them, glancing back once to see Stan talking to Hattie.

She turned to see Nick standing by himself near a window and watching her approach. She tingled from the look in his green eyes.

He could set her on fire with just a look, and for a moment, she forgot everyone else. Nick's gaze held hers as she walked closer. She wanted to just walk into his embrace, but this wasn't the time to do so.

"Stan said you wanted to see me."

"Do I ever," he said in a husky voice. "You are even sexy just walking across the room."

Her pulse jumped and she drew a deep breath. He took her arm. "Come here. I want to show you something."

"We're leaving them?"

"Just for a minute. C'mon." They left the room, stepped across the hall into a formal living room, and he closed the door. Because of heavy pale blue silk drapes, less light came into the room. It was the east side of the house, so the late-afternoon sunlight did not spill into the room. She looked at Nick expectantly.

"Actually, I told Stan to go entertain Hattie and Grandmother, and I told my other brothers to find something to do for a few minutes. I wanted to be alone with you because you look incredible."

"Nick," she said, laughing and tingling from his compliment, "thank you, but we need to get back. I just got introduced to your family. We can't disappear and— Don't you dare kiss me and get me all mussed up when I've just met them," she admonished when he came closer.

"You really don't want me to kiss you?" he asked in a husky tone while he lightly caressed her nape.

All teasing had vanished, replaced by desire in his green eyes, and her heart thudded. She couldn't tell him she didn't want him to kiss her. Words failed her, and besides, she'd be lying if she said that. Right now, like always, all she wanted was to step into his arms and kiss him. Desire flared as she looked up and saw his hungry expression.

"Ah, Nick, I can't say no to you. Not when you look at me like that. You're going to—"

"Yeah, I am," he interrupted and pulled her tightly against him, his mouth coming down on hers.

Sensations rocked her, centering low inside her, hot and insistent, making her want him totally. She wanted his kisses, his caresses, his hands and body on her, his thick erection inside her. She wrapped her arms around him, stood on her toes and let her kiss tell him her desires.

She didn't know how long they kissed, but when she felt his hand at the back of her dress where her zipper started, she leaned away.

"Nick, wait. There's a family dinner out there. We need to go back and I need to pull myself together."

He stared at her while he took deep breaths. "You're right. I'll cool down. You make me forget everything else. Let's go back together. Hell, we're getting married soon. If we sneak off to kiss, that's not shocking."

"It is to me," she said and he smiled.

"I think that's my line. I didn't feel anything for a long time until I met you."

"Actually, while I haven't been bogged down in grief, I haven't felt anything for a long time, either. This is mutual," she said.

"It has been from the first moment we met and that's another shock," he replied. He took her hand and led her to the door. "Come on—let's see how Grandmother and Hattie are getting along."

"I think quite well or we'd hear Hattie."

He smiled and slipped his arm around her waist to give her a squeeze. "This marriage of convenience is the best idea I've had in a long time."

She wondered if he was reminding her so she wouldn't forget that it was a loveless marriage. She didn't care because this marriage made her Hattie's mother instantly. Stepmom at first, but he'd agreed about the adoption. She couldn't wait to get the process going.

Nick stopped and turned to her. He ran his finger back and forth on her wrist lightly, a casual touch, yet it made her pulse beat faster. "Before we join the others, can I get you something to drink? Wine, beer, mixed drink, margarita?"

"I'll take white wine," she said.

"Fine. Go ahead and join them. I'll get our drinks."

He walked her back to the room where she saw the brothers seated around Myra and Hattie. Stan sat close to his grandmother and held Hattie on his lap. She heard Hattie laughing and knew all was well.

"I think your grandmother is going to approve of Hattie," she whispered to Nick.

"I think she'll adore her. You just watch."

As Talia walked in to join the group, all the men came to their feet.

"Please be seated," Talia said, taking a chair offered by Adam. For a few moments she watched Nick's family interact with Hattie and felt herself begin to relax.

"You have a beautiful little girl who looks like the Duncans," Myra said to Nick as he joined them and handed a glass of white wine to Talia. He held a bottle of beer in his other hand.

"Her mother always said she was an easy baby, ready to smile and seldom fussy," Talia said. "She's stayed that way in spite of what she's been through."

"Ahh, we're going to get called to dinner," Nick said, looking up as his cook, Kirby, appeared at the door to announce dinner. Nick scooped up the pink bunny and picked up Hattie from his brother. "I'll put her in her chair."

At the dinner table, Nick sat at one end and Myra at another. Talia sat on Nick's right and Hattie sat between them in an old-fashioned wooden high chair that Nick said he and his brothers had used and their mother before them.

Throughout dinner she was constantly aware of Nick, laughing with him and with his brothers as they told stories of their antics on the ranch while growing up. It seemed he felt the same. His gaze never strayed far from her. Not for the first time, she thought about the night to come. She yearned for the kisses that were sure to come. No doubt there'd be more than kisses, and that thought made her want to be alone with him right now. Forever.

With a start she realized her biggest fear was coming true: she was in danger of falling in love with him, something that could only mean heartbreak. The minute that thought came, she pushed it aside. None of this marriage to Nick Duncan could be a mistake, she told herself. Because she would get to be Hattie's stepmom and then her legal mother if the adoption went through. That made this the most wonderful marriage possible.

Later in the evening Talia stood at the bar with Nick. "Your grandmother and your brothers have held Hattie all evening. Stan just put her in your grandmother's lap again. I better go see if she's okay with that."

Catching her wrist lightly, Nick drew Talia back. "The guys will watch Hattie, and Grandmother probably told them to put Hattie in her lap. My grandmother is so happy to finally have another little grandchild to dote on."

"She seems happy with Hattie and, surprisingly enough, she's been friendly to me and I'm glad."

"It's obvious she loves Hattie, so there is no battle there. I think my grandmother is going to love every minute you and Hattie are at the ranch. She's not the only one," he said and she smiled at him while her heart skipped a beat.

"I think this is going to be good, Nick. It's going to give me my dream, so I'll go into our marriage happier than I've ever been in my life."

"I'm glad. It may be a loveless marriage, but we're friends, and physically, we'll be lovers. That's a fantastic surprise," he said, his voice getting deeper while desire filled his green eyes. He took a step closer to her. "I'm ready for the others to go home so we can be alone. I've looked forward to tonight and not because of having the family visit."

His words made her tingle. Her gaze ran across his broad shoulders, then back to his mouth. Finally, she met his knowing gaze and she could feel the heat in her cheeks and knew she blushed.

"We better change the subject, Nick."

"This is the best possible subject, talking about kissing you and holding you in my arms. I may run them all off soon."

"Don't do that. It's my first visit and I need to go back and get to know them."

"You will. They think Hattie is fun or they wouldn't be hanging around her like they are. I know my brothers. They think you're gorgeous, so they'll come see you. You'll get to know them, I promise. Tonight I want your attention," he said in a husky voice that made her blood heat up and made her forget the others.

"Watch out, Nick. When you're being so appealing, so sexy, you may complicate our relationship. Neither of us wants that."

"No. I don't need another damn complication in my life or another big emotional upheaval. Not at all. But I think we can avoid that happening and still have a great married life," he said in a sexy, husky tone that played over her and made her tingle as much as if he had caressed her. She hadn't known Nick long, but she could tell he was intent on seduction.

"We better break this up," she said breathlessly, unable to hide her feelings. "We have company, and we need to give them attention."

He looked amused. "I will right now if you promise we can come back to this conversation."

She tilted her head to gaze up at him and ran her finger lightly over the back of his hand. "Of course we'll come back to the subject of seduction. You can count on that," she said in a soft, sultry voice.

He drew a deep breath, desire flashing in his expression. "Damn. I'd like to carry you off with me right now."

"Instead, let's go talk to your family," she said, walking past him, wondering if he guessed how fast her heart beat or how hot she felt. She wanted his kisses, wanted his hands on her, and knew that was what would happen after they got Hattie to bed. She could hardly wait.

Stan was the last to leave. At the door, he turned to Nick and glanced down at the baby asleep in his

"4 for 4" MINI-SURVEY

We are prepared to **REWARD** you with 2 FREE books and 2 FREE gifts for completing our MINI SURVEY!

FREE Value Over $20!

You'll get...

TWO FREE BOOKS & TWO FREE GIFTS

just for participating in our Mini Survey!

Dear Reader,

IT'S A FACT: if you answer 4 quick questions, we'll send you 4 FREE REWARDS!

I'm not kidding you. As a leading publisher of women's fiction, we value your opinions... and your time. That's why we are prepared to **reward** you handsomely for completing our mini-survey. In fact, we have 4 Free Rewards for you, including 2 free books and 2 free gifts.

As you may have guessed, that's why our mini-survey is called **"4 for 4".** Answer 4 questions and get 4 Free Rewards. It's that simple!

Thank you for participating in our survey,

Pam Powers

To get your 4 FREE REWARDS:
Complete the survey below and return the insert today to receive 2 FREE BOOKS and 2 FREE GIFTS guaranteed!

"4 for 4" MINI-SURVEY

1 Is reading one of your favorite hobbies?
YES ☐ NO ☐

2 Do you prefer to read instead of watch TV?
YES ☐ NO ☐

3 Do you read newspapers and magazines?
YES ☐ NO ☐

4 Do you enjoy trying new book series with FREE BOOKS?
YES ☐ NO ☐

YES! I have completed the above Mini-Survey. Please send me my 4 FREE REWARDS (worth over $20 retail). I understand that I am under no obligation to buy anything, as explained on the back of this card.

225/326 HDL GMYG

FIRST NAME

LAST NAME

ADDRESS

APT.#

CITY

STATE/PROV.

ZIP/POSTAL CODE

▲ If offer card is missing write to: Reader Service, P.O. Box 1341, Buffalo, NY 14240-8531 or visit www.ReaderService.com ▲

BUSINESS REPLY MAIL

FIRST-CLASS MAIL   PERMIT NO. 717   BUFFALO, NY

POSTAGE WILL BE PAID BY ADDRESSEE

READER SERVICE
PO BOX 1341
BUFFALO NY 14240-8571

NO POSTAGE
NECESSARY
IF MAILED
IN THE
UNITED STATES

arms. "You have a sweet little daughter there, Nick. I think I'm going to like being an uncle again."

"I'm glad. She seems to like you."

Stan smiled. "She likes everybody. She won Grandmother over."

Stan turned to Talia. "We're happy to have you joining the family, Talia, and it was a good dinner, my brother."

"Thanks, Stan. For a bachelor, you do all right with little kids."

"What can I say? It's my experience with calves," Stan replied, grinning as he walked out the door.

The minute they were alone, Talia asked, "Want me to take Hattie?"

"No. I'll carry her to bed and then you can take over."

She followed him upstairs, treading softly so as to not wake the baby. "Thanks, Nick, for introducing me to your family. They were great and I'm so happy to get to know them."

"My brothers and I are close, so after we marry, you'll probably see them often. Grandmother will be good to Hattie and she'll shower her with too much stuff."

Talia laughed. "Says the man who has already given Hattie a pink bunny, her first present from a Duncan."

"I can promise you there will be more to come. Besides, you can't spoil a baby. You can a kid, but not a baby. To my way of thinking, a baby should be showered with love."

"Aw, Nick, that's nice," she said, thinking it might be even more difficult than she had thought to resist falling in love with him. "Don't get too nice. Even though you've given me Hattie, I don't want to fall in love because I know you never will."

"That's right," he said, suddenly sounding somber, his voice getting deeper. "I'm glad you're okay with that."

"I am," she replied. "I'm not looking for love, either. It didn't work out too well last time. I don't want a repeat of what I went through with my ex-husband. All I can hope for is that we're compatible. So far, so good," she said. Truthfully, they were more than compatible, she thought. His slightest touch set her heart pounding.

Right now she had a heart-racing awareness of him so close beside her. Since their kiss, she had been far more conscious of him when they were together. Now they were together, alone, late at night in his ranch house after a fun evening. She thought about the kiss they had shared and felt her pulse race.

She opened the door to her suite and Nick entered, placing Hattie in her crib. He settled her then turned to Talia. "At this point you take charge. Do what you need to do and come back down so we can talk awhile and maybe make a few plans about our wedding. The sooner we get married, the better."

"I agree with that. There's one thing, Nick… You're a wealthy man, but this is a marriage of convenience, so just a plain wedding band will suffice for me. I don't need an engagement ring because we're not going to be engaged more than a few days. I really mean it. A big ring won't be significant to either one of us. Let's let that one go."

He smiled at her. "Talia, I think there are few women in the world who would have made that speech to me. That's fine with me if you're good with it."

She nodded. "I won't be long. I just want to be sure she's down," she said, nodding at Hattie.

"Want something to drink?"

"Ice water would be nice, thank you."

"You've got it," he said and left.

She quickly changed into comfortable clothes and checked again on Hattie, who'd barely stirred. She looked down at her sleeping and smiled at the thought of how Hattie had been welcomed into a family who would love her. She and Hattie were both fortunate. She had one more week now until the semester ended. When that happened, she and Nick would marry.

A tingle went up her spine at the thought. Was it from anticipation…or apprehension?

She hoped she wasn't headed for more heartache. Nick would not fall in love, and she didn't want to fall in love with a man who had no love in his heart for her. She simply had to guard her heart.

But living with an appealing, handsome Texas rancher who, based on his kiss, was the sexiest man she had ever known… Well, it might be easier said than done.

Six

It seemed no time at all that it was June and she was standing at Nick's side, repeating vows. She wore a short pale blue linen dress with a V-neck and straight skirt. Her hair was gathered and fastened with clips high on the back of her head, long curls falling freely in back. Nick had sent her a corsage of white orchids pinned on one shoulder of her dress. They stood at the altar in a small chapel in Nick's large Dallas church with his family in attendance. There was a very small group for the service, and she was relieved that they hadn't planned a big reception afterward.

When Nick slipped the gold wedding band on her finger, she looked at the ring that signified she was Hattie's legal stepmother. A rush of gratitude and joy filled her.

When it came time for Nick to kiss her, she met his gaze. His green eyes looked frosty and he barely glanced at her before he brushed his lips briefly against hers. Then they were introduced as Mr. and Mrs. Nicholas Duncan and the ceremony was over. One glance at him and she knew he hurt. This wedding was bringing back memories for him, making him miss his wife and baby son.

Nick had had his first wedding here, although it was in the sanctuary, not the little chapel. She was sure he was being bombarded by memories.

Today he wore a charcoal suit, a white dress shirt with French cuffs and gold links, his black boots and a sterling bolo tie. He looked incredibly handsome, but his somber countenance made her feel sad for him.

"Thank you, Nick," she said as she turned to him.

"I think I need to say thank you. You'll be good for Hattie and I won't have to worry constantly about her. In my family she will be showered with love."

"I'm glad she will be," Talia said, but she wondered if he even heard her. He seemed preoccupied, wrapped up in memories.

He took her arm and they turned for a picture. Originally they had agreed to skip the pictures, but then reconsidered so that Hattie would have them to look at someday and think they were happily married.

They went back to his Dallas house for a reception.

Even with just his family and a few very close Dallas friends of theirs, she guessed there were over twenty people at his house. Nick had carried Hattie almost the whole first hour they were there, showing her to people and introducing her. She couldn't keep her eyes from seeking him out across the room. What was it about him that drew her? From the very first moment, he had seemed sexy, exciting. Right now, in her view, Nick was the most handsome man in the room. Especially holding a baby.

Hattie had a pink dress with little embroidered rosebuds and a pale green matching sash. She wore a locket that had been Myra's when she was a child. Her hair was in ringlets with a pink bow that had two small rosebuds.

Inviting smells came from the kitchen and they welcomed their guests to a delicious buffet. There were small tables in the family room and on the patio, and extra staff had been hired to help serve. Nick had hired Paula Fletcher, Kirby's wife, to watch Hattie, wanting Talia to be free to enjoy her wedding day. Taking care of Hattie had never seemed a chore to her, especially today. She was Hattie's stepmom now and Nick had promised that Monday morning they would start the adoption process. They had already met with his attorney, who had filed the petition for adoption. Nick's money would move the whole procedure along faster and she was giddy with joy.

In the afternoon a moment came when Talia finally sneaked away from the guests, standing alone by a table that held slices of wedding cake. She wasn't alone for long.

"We have a beautiful little girl," Nick said, appearing at her side.

His words thrilled her. "That sounds wonderful. I can't ever tell you how thrilled I am, Nick," she said, glancing around him. "I left Hattie with you, so who has her now?"

"Paula's watching her, but the family is entertaining her. None of us will let her toddle off."

"I'm glad you got a fence for your swimming pool," she said, glancing out the window to the backyard.

"Let's not worry about Hattie right now," he said, pulling her against him to kiss passionately.

Her heart thudded and all she could think about was Nick, her husband. She wrapped her arms around his neck and clung to him, kissing him in return, feeling as if she was on fire with longing.

"Did I tell you how beautiful you look today?" he asked in a husky voice when he broke the kiss.

She smiled at him. "You did."

"I'll say it again. You're a beautiful bride."

"Thank you. You're a very handsome groom," she said lightly. She would never tell him that when she first saw him waiting at the altar, he had taken her breath away. He'd looked like a celebrity, handsome, sexy and exciting.

Then she remembered how his look had changed.

"I'm sorry, Nick, if this is making you remember your first wedding and if it's stirring up old hurts."

"I live with those hurts on a daily basis, so this is nothing new. Life is filled with constant reminders of Regina and Artie. Each day, each month, I think how old Artie would be. And I won't lie. This has made me think about my wedding with Regina."

She felt her heart tighten in sympathy. But before she could offer him comfort, he changed the subject.

"But I'm more worried about you," he said. "You're getting cheated today. You should be marrying a man who loves you and who you love. I hope someday Hattie looks back and realizes how much you loved her and how much you sacrificed personally so you could be a mother to her. When she's old enough, I'll tell her, but right now that seems eons away. You've made a giant sacrifice to give her your love and be a mother to her."

"It's no sacrifice, Nick. To be her mother was my dream. She's so precious. I'll always be grateful to you," she said and meant it.

She put her hands on his chest, feeling the rock-hard muscles from his physical work on the ranch. "I want to give you something in return, Nick. I want to make you happy. I want us to be happy together and I want this marriage to be good for both of us," she said.

He looked down at her and she couldn't read the expression on his handsome face. For a moment she thought to ask him what he was thinking, but then he finally spoke.

"I don't think it's going to be a task to be happy together, Talia. And I'm sure the marriage will be good for both of us." The smile he gave her didn't quite reach his eyes, but she returned it anyway.

This was one of the happiest days of her life. She only wished Nick could feel the same way.

She could hardly believe how things had worked out. She was getting to raise Hattie as a stay-at-home mom, like she'd always wanted. Her resignation had already been accepted by the college. And despite her objections, Nick had set up her and Hattie with incredibly generous trusts that would ensure their financial safety for life.

Once again, as she had done at the altar hours ago, she vowed to make her new husband just as happy.

They rejoined their guests, and by midafternoon the only ones left were Nick's brothers. They sat on the patio and Nick seemed to be enjoying their time, so Talia slipped away to put Hattie down for a nap.

When she came down, Adam and Blake had gone and Stan was saying goodbye. As usual, he was the last to leave.

"Well, we did it," Nick said when he closed the door behind Stan. He placed his hands on her shoulders. "You're now Mrs. Duncan and the stepmother of a little fourteen-month-old toddler."

She was aware of his hands, lightly moving back and forth on her shoulders and setting fires in their paths.

She was his wife. And she was ready to love him tonight the way only a wife could.

Warning bells went off in her head, but she ignored them. A sexual relationship wouldn't sweep her into falling in love with him. Or was she fooling herself and already sliding down a slippery slope into being in love with her handsome, appealing new husband?

It was after ten when they finally tucked a sleeping Hattie into bed for the night. Because of her late nap, she hadn't been ready to go down at her usual bedtime. Once Talia placed her in the crib, Nick slipped his arm around her waist. "Come have a drink with me and let's sit and talk. I couldn't go to sleep now if I tried."

"Sure," she answered, smiling at him.

He walked her out of the suite, not taking his hands off her. He wanted Talia in his arms, wanted to carry her off to his bed. She excited him and enticed him. But guilt stopped him cold. It shook him because he felt all his loyalty and love should be with memories of the life he'd had with Regina, his best friend until her death. Talia and Hattie would never displace memories of Regina and Artie or replace his love for them, but he still felt guilty for wanting Talia.

He'd thought he was beginning to mend, but today had set him back. The loss of his first wife and son still hurt and it hurt badly.

While Talia knew there was no love between them, that theirs was strictly a marriage of convenience, she should have had a better day. He'd planned to make it so, but when this morning came, he didn't want to do anything except get through the ceremony and the day.

He was glad for Talia, who was happy because now there was no danger of losing Hattie. She deserved that and Hattie should be with Talia, someone who would pour out love and be a good mother. He was certain Talia would be that.

As they walked down the steps together, he couldn't get it off his conscience that he should have done better for her sake. She shouldn't be marrying out of convenience. She should have someone who loved her. A beautiful woman, Talia deserved a man who would shower her with love and attention. Nick felt guilty about Talia, and for other reasons, he felt guilty about Regina.

He and Talia had touched casually, lightly, off and on all day long. They'd held hands and repeated vows. But where was it leading? He glanced at Talia. She wasn't going to have a real marriage…but did she want a real wedding night? There was one way to find out.

* * *

"We've got the monitors in the family room to hear her if she should wake. Let's go have that drink."

The video monitor had been one of her earliest purchases. Talia had one in her small house, but here, in the Dallas mansion, it was a necessity.

"Fine, Nick, if you really want to. If you're doing that because you feel you should for me, don't," she said. She knew he was hurting and still wrapped up in memories of when he had married the first time.

He smiled at her. "I'm doing it because I want to be with you."

"I won't argue with that, then."

As they went downstairs, she was intensely aware of his hand on the small of her back. She cast a glance at him. He had shed his jacket and tie, and the first couple of buttons on his shirt were unfastened. After the long day, his hair was tousled, begging her to reach out and smooth it. She had to admit he looked sexy, too appealing, and she could think of many things she'd rather be doing with him than talking.

When they went into the family room she saw a bucket of ice with a bottle in it. Surprised, she walked across the room with him, pulled it out and read the label. "Champagne? Where and when did this arrive?"

"I had Kirby put it out for us," Nick said, taking the bottle from her. When he popped the cork, he picked up a delicate crystal flute and poured the pale, bubbling champagne in first one flute to hand to her and then into the other flute. When he put the bottle back on ice, he turned to look at her and raised his glass.

"Here's to our marriage. Even though it is a marriage of convenience, may it be happy and may we be wed a long time." She touched her flute to his with a ring of crystal against crystal and they both sipped their champagne. When she looked at him, she realized he was paying attention to her now, gazing at her intently. Gone was the shuttered expression he'd had through the ceremony and most of the day.

She held up her flute. "May this marriage bring you the joy and happiness it's bringing to me."

He touched her flute and they sipped again. He turned to pick up the remote to turn on music and then he set his glass of champagne on the table and took hers from her. He stepped close to take her hand and draw her closer as he began to dance to the ballad with her.

"It was hard for me to get through today," he whispered against her ear. "You knew it was and you were so good about it."

He held her away to look into her eyes as they danced. "I should have made a bigger effort to hide those feelings," he told her. "I loved Regina with all my heart. I can't just shut that off. In some ways I feel as if I'm betraying her. Common sense makes me know that I'm not, but I can't stop feeling that way. And Arthur. I loved my son."

"You don't need to explain loving them," she said, feeling his pain, yet touched that he was trying to explain it. "I understand that." She'd certainly cried buckets of tears over losing her parents and her two unborn babies.

"I couldn't keep from getting carried back and thinking about my wedding with Regina."

"I really do understand."

"I know you do, Talia, and you were wonderful about it." He gestured to the champagne. "This is just my way of saying thank you." He twirled her around the family room in time to the soft music, then dipped her back over his arm when the love song ended. His gaze drifted over her, from her face down past her breasts, and it was as if he had lightly caressed her instead of giving her just a look.

Her heart thudded so hard, she thought he could hear it in the silence before the next song started.

His eyes settled on her lips and she thought he was about to kiss her. Instead, he whispered something she wasn't sure he intended her to hear. "You should have had more."

She straightened and framed his face with her hands. "Nick, stop worrying that we're not in love and I'm not marrying a man who loves me. Today you gave me what I wanted most in my whole life— that sweet child I love as if she were my own."

"No, I only partially did," he said, looking solemn. "I gave you what you wanted, but I've been in love, Talia. I married for love and had a baby we both loved. That's a whole lot more. It creates a world filled with joy and happiness during a wedding day and honeymoon. I couldn't give you that."

"But I'm happy, Nick, so stop worrying."

He opened his mouth to object, but she covered his lips with one finger. "Nick, life is filled with risks. We both took risks today. I took the risk of this 'convenient' marriage and I got what I wanted. You took the risk of marrying me and you got someone to care for Hattie. And I intend to do just that for the next eighteen years, give or take a year or two."

He gave her a searching stare as she lowered her hand. "How is it possible that I got so lucky finding you? Or rather that you found me. I'm so grateful for you, Talia." He took her hands in his and stepped back to sweep her with a glance, his eyes searing her flesh through her clothes. "Now that I can lay my conscience to rest, I want to say, you look stunning in your beautiful blue dress."

"Thank you," she said, smiling at him. "You look quite handsome yourself." She meant the compliment, despite the fact that at the same time she was trying to deny his appeal. She had to, because it'd be too easy to fall for this amazing, sexy, handsome man. She couldn't fool herself into thinking that he was happy about their arrangement. Surely he'd have preferred to go on his way, to live his life without including her in it. But she was part of it now, and as long as he was a good daddy for Hattie, Talia would be happy. She just hoped she could guard her heart enough so that she never lost it to Nick, because he was still in love with his late wife.

When the music started again, Nick stepped toward her. She thought he'd take her in his arms and resume the dance, but instead, his gaze settled on her lips. He inhaled deeply as his eyes met hers again—and she saw it.

Desire.

It blazed there in his green eyes, which had darkened to emerald.

While her heart began to drum, his arm tightened around her waist to draw her to him. "You're gorgeous, sexy and appealing, and it's time you know you're appreciated on more than one level," he said in a husky voice. As he held her tightly against his solid length, he leaned down, slowly, inch by inch, stealing her breath until finally his mouth covered hers. His tongue met hers in a slow dance, a tantalizing torment that made her tremble. Moaning, she wrapped her arms around his neck and kissed him in return.

She forgot all the reasons to be cautious with him. At the moment she just wanted his kisses, his hard body pressed against hers, his hands on her. She had danced with him today, laughed with him, married him, and now she finally could kiss him. And she did.

His kisses were sexier than she had ever experienced, this man who had made her biggest dream come true. It was a combination that was too enticing to resist. This handsome rancher had taken away her fears and worries about losing Hattie, had married her today. Tonight she wanted him—totally. She wanted his kisses, his body against hers, his hands on her. He must have read her mind, because as he continued to hold her close with one hand, his other hand trailed slowly down her back, over her bottom. Even through her clothes she could feel his caresses as he touched the backs of her thighs and then up her legs to her waist. While he kissed her, she felt his fingers at the buttons on the front of her dress. When she reached up to close her hand over his, he raised his head to give her a questioning look.

"We don't have to go to bed together tonight," she whispered. "There's a lot of time ahead of us. You've had an emotional day and I have, too, so if you're doing this out of a sense of duty, you don't need to do so."

He smiled as he unfastened a button. "Talia, I promise you, there is absolutely not one tiny shred of feeling that I have a duty to perform here," he remarked drily and she could hear the amusement in his voice. He unfastened another button, pushed the dress open and ran his warm finger lightly on the rise of her breast. "This isn't a chore for me," he said as his smile faded and his voice became hoarse, breathless.

"You'll complicate our lives from the first night we're together," she warned.

"I might do that," he said, his hungry gaze making her heart pound. "We complicated it when we married and we knew we had complicated it after that first kiss."

"Nick," she whispered, unaware of even moving as his arm wrapped around her waist and he drew her tightly against him. Her gaze flew to his mouth while her heart thudded. She couldn't deny it. She wanted his naked body against hers. They were married, man and wife, and she wanted it all with him, and at the moment she was reckless and eager enough to risk her heart.

"Nick, I want you, but I'm warning you, my body comes with a heart inside and emotions all tangled with sex. You're taking a risk here just as much as I am."

"After hearing your first words before your warning, I'm willing to take the risks," he whispered gruffly as he showered kisses on her throat and down her neck, onto her breasts.

"You've been warned," she whispered. "I'm not going to argue with you. I want you, and I have since that first kiss."

That may have been what Nick needed to hear, because he ran his tongue over her peaked nipple while he cupped her breast in his hand. Talia couldn't stifle the gasp that escaped her lips.

"You're so soft," he whispered. "Just to touch you is magic."

She framed his face with her hands, feeling the stubble on his jaw against her palms. "Nick, no one has ever kissed me the way you do. I suspect no one has ever made love to me the way you will. I want you to take all night," she said, certain that he was finally seeing her in the moment, that he was not lost in memories. He had come into the present and she was waiting, wanting him. "I want to kiss and touch you just as much as I want your hands and mouth on every inch of me."

"Sounds like the best possible plan," he whispered gruffly as he kissed her throat. Peeling away the top of her dress, he brushed more kisses down her slender neck. "Right now, I want you and I want to kiss and touch you for hours. We have all night to pleasure each other, to discover what we like." He straightened to gaze into her eyes and the desire she saw there sent delicious shivers up her spine. When his gaze lowered to her mouth, she couldn't get her breath. Then, finally, he tightened his arm around her waist and drew her to him to kiss her.

His mouth covered hers, his tongue heightening her desire while he kissed her. She wanted more of him, wanted him to make her forget everything else except their lovemaking. Passion spilled over her, setting her ablaze.

She unbuttoned his shirt and pushed it away to let it fall. As soon as it was gone, she showered kisses on his broad shoulder, running her fingers through the thick mat of curls on his chest. Her hands were at his belt, and in seconds, she pulled it free and dropped it while he continued to peel away her clothing until she was wearing only lacy bikini panties. He held her hips and stepped back a fraction to look at her.

"From the first moment I saw you, I knew you were beautiful. You're perfection," he said in a gruff voice, his gaze consuming her. "You make my heart race and my breathing difficult. You're gorgeous." He slid his hands down over her hips, pushing away the panties till they fell around her feet and she stepped out of them. He ran his hands lightly over her, starting at her throat, down over each breast, caressing her slowly, cupping her breasts and circling each tip with his tongue. He straightened, still watching her with half-closed eyes, as his hands drifted down, one sliding slowly over her belly while his other hand skimmed over her bottom.

She gasped with pleasure and clung to his hips as his hands drifted to her thighs.

"This is magic, Talia. You make me want you every way possible."

He tossed aside the last of his clothes. His body against hers was hot, hard and exciting, making her tremble with eagerness and discovery as she ran her hands and trailed her lips over him.

Her fingers explored lower, over his flat, muscled stomach, down on his thighs, and then she stroked his throbbing manhood that made her insides clench and heat. She wanted him inside her. She wanted to give herself, to feel that he was part of her, as close as they could get.

"Nick, I want you—"

"Shh, just wait. We're just getting started. I want to pleasure you, to stir you to heights, to discover what you like best, to taste and thrill you," he whispered as he filled his hands with her soft, full breasts. His fingers circled each taut peak slowly, deliberately, sending showers of tingling sensations following the faintest touch. Her breasts felt swollen, aching for his mouth, and she yearned for him to come inside her, to move together, to finally reach a climax together. She felt driven, need building with each stroke of his fingers, each slow lick of his wet tongue.

"Ahh, Nick," she gasped with pleasure, running her hands over his narrow hips, taking his thick rod in her hand to stroke and caress him. She rubbed against him and then ran her tongue slowly, intimately, where her hand had been.

He closed his eyes and wound his hand in her hair, holding her while he groaned with pleasure and desire. He pulled her up to him suddenly to kiss her hard, a demanding, possessive kiss that revealed he wanted her with an equally desperate urgency. His hungry kiss made her heart beat even faster. It was a kiss of possession that drove her wild with longing for all of him.

"Nick, the bed," she whispered.

"Soon," he answered, his hands drifting down to her silky inner thighs and then rubbing her intimately as she cried out and clung to him.

Kissing her, he scooped her up into his strong arms and carried her upstairs to his bedroom. He yanked away the covers and placed her on the bed. While he kissed her, he moved between her legs and then he looked down at her.

"You're beautiful. Every inch of you is so beautiful," he whispered.

She reached for him, but he pushed her hands away. He put her legs over his shoulders, giving him more access while he toyed with her, stroked her, set her on fire with longing.

Sensations bombarded her, driving her to move, to cry out for more of him as she shifted and knelt before him. She took his thick rod in her hand, exciting him as he had her.

He rolled her over on her stomach, running his hands over her and then his tongue while she writhed in pleasure and need beneath him. With a cry, she rolled over and sat up to kiss him, wrapping her long legs around him and pulling him down while she fell back on the bed. He retrieved a condom from the nightstand drawer and knelt between her legs to put it on.

"I want you now," she whispered, gazing into his eyes.

He entered her slowly, partially, pausing and then withdrawing and driving her wild.

"Nick, I want you now."

He entered her, filling her with his hot, thick manhood, then withdrawing while he kissed her. She arched beneath him, pulling at his firm butt, tightening her legs around him to draw him closer. "Nick, I want you, all of you," she whispered, pulling on him.

Finally he filled her, his manhood hot and thick. She moved her hips beneath him. "Love me," she gasped, wanting him desperately, tugging at him.

He kissed her, a kiss that made her breasts tingle and become more sensitive to the touch of his chest against them. She tried to pull him closer, arching her hips to meet his every thrust as he began to pump faster. With a cry of ecstasy and need, she met him and moved with him. His thrusts filled her, faster and more intense, until she shattered with a wild climax, arching beneath him, her cry muffled by his kiss. Seconds later he found his own release.

Still, he continued to thrust into her. She felt need build again inside her and clutched his broad shoulders, moving in perfect rhythm with him. In seconds he had her crying out while she shuddered in a powerful orgasm. Even in her ecstasy she felt him reach his climax, pounding into her with one final thrust.

"Ahh, Talia," he whispered on a ragged breath. "You have to be the sexiest woman on earth."

She held him tightly. Smiling, she couldn't answer. She was sunk in euphoria, satiated, enveloped in rapture, and she didn't want to speak or think or do anything except relish the moment and his body, his weight on her a reassurance that he was real and in her arms. He raised his head slightly to look at her. "You're not speaking. Are you all right?"

"I'm more than all right. I didn't know it could ever be that great. It's an effort to talk, an effort to think. I feel as if every bone in my body melted and I don't want to get out of this bed or let go of you ever."

He chuckled softly, a rumble in his chest causing her to feel the vibrations. "I hope you don't get out of this bed tonight. It was terribly shortsighted of me to think we wouldn't want any kind of wedding night to ourselves, not to mention dismissing all thoughts of a honeymoon."

"A honeymoon seemed a ridiculous thing to plan when we not only aren't in love, we didn't ever really plan to make love tonight. I feel too exhausted to talk about it."

He showered kisses on her face. "Well, it was shortsighted on my part because I knew what it was like to kiss you and I knew how beautiful and sexy you are. I guess I really have been numb to the world for a long time. Numb in all parts from my brain down."

She smiled. "You were far from numb tonight." She snuggled against his hot body. "Just stay here in my arms and hold me close and I'll be happy."

"That I can do, my dear."

She didn't know how long they lay in each other's

arms, but finally he spoke softly, his deep voice making vibrations in his chest. "Talia, tonight was spectacular, mind-blowing sex, hot and urgent, but I can't promise that it will be a buffer to keep away the hurt and pain of losses that I have. I'll still have moments. Hopefully, if I work at it, I can control my hurt and keep my low moments from dragging things down for you."

"Don't worry. I've told you how I feel. It's all worth it for what I get out of this marriage—Hattie as my daughter. And when you get to know her, you'll be a loving dad for her. I know you will. I can't ask for anything more. The rest is icing on the cake, and believe me, this hot, mind-boggling sex with you is better than the usual icing on the cake."

He rolled beside her, pulled her close and lay on his side to face her. He ran his fingers through her hair to comb it away from her face.

"The day will come, I'm sure, when I'll love little Hattie the way I loved Artie."

She heard the sorrow, as well as the hope, in his voice. "I'm so sorry for your losses, Nick. You probably thought you had everything in the world you wanted and it was all taken from you. If I had lost Hattie like I thought I was going to, I'd be far worse than you've been. When I thought the state might take her, I couldn't sleep or eat. Thanks to you that isn't going to happen, but believe me, I understand your hurt and can accept that."

He leaned down to kiss her forehead tenderly.

"I'm lucky. Hattie can't ever take Artie's place, but she'll have her own place."

They lay in each other's arms quietly, till Nick spoke again. "This is good, Talia. Very good," he whispered against her. "Thank you again for being you and for understanding today."

"I told you—you've given me what I wanted the most. Few people can ever say that to someone else. You've made me a very happy woman, Nick."

"I'm glad."

They became silent and she realized there were no words of love, no easy banter after fantastic sex. The day had been an emotional roller coaster for him and somewhat for her, as well. But they had gotten through it better than she had expected.

They had gotten through it with his family welcoming her and now she was Mrs. Nicholas Duncan. Nick's wife and Hattie's mother. She turned to share her joy with Nick and saw that his eyes were closed, but she didn't think he was asleep. As if he knew what she was thinking, he reached out and slipped his arm around her, pulling her close against him and turning slightly so he could hug her.

"You've been great today," he said.

"Thanks," she whispered, wrapping her arms around him and wondering if she should leave right now and get in her own bed. She started to move away but he tightened his arm around her, so she settled back. The monitor for Hattie was right beside the bed, so she snuggled against Nick and closed her eyes.

The next thing she knew, she stirred because Nick was talking and holding her tightly. "Regina, Regina," he mumbled.

Seven

Startled, Talia came fully awake. She realized Nick was dreaming and he must mean his late wife, Regina. "Nick," she whispered.

Sitting up suddenly and breathing heavily, he looked around the bedroom.

"Nick, you were dreaming."

He stared at her and she wondered if he even remembered that he had married only hours earlier.

He rubbed the back of his neck. "Sorry."

She slipped out of bed and grabbed up her dress. "I think I'll check on Hattie and stay in my room."

She left his bedroom, closing the door behind her, unable to deny the disappointment that enveloped her. He hadn't asked her to come back or to stay. Had he woken remembering his dream about his first wife? Or when tomorrow came, would he even remember dreaming?

Able to see because of a little night-light, she entered her suite and crossed the room to Hattie's crib. As she looked at her, her heart filled with joy. She loved Hattie and now she could be her mother. She couldn't be angry with Nick for mourning the woman he loved or the little baby boy he lost. Time would help him heal to a point, but there would always be memories that hurt, always be a void. If dreams came about his first wife, he couldn't stop them. She could understand his pain and regretted he was sad when their wedding had showered her with happiness. She felt as he got to know Hattie, the love for her would help to alleviate his pain.

She climbed into her bed and hoped Nick slept peacefully. The fantastic sex was one more thing that would cause them to bond. She didn't expect Nick to fall in love with her, but life could still be good if she just didn't fall deeply in love with him and need his love in her life. That was the one thing that could lead to a broken heart. If she could just take the sex the way he did, without emotional ties, without falling in love, then they would have a good relationship. Could she do that? Could she keep her feelings from getting involved?

Common sense told her to keep up her guard, but the way she reacted when he held her or when he kissed her told her it wouldn't be easy. Nick was far too charming. She sighed and shook her head. Could she keep him at arm's length all the time? Did she even want to? They were married, after all. Winning Nick's love might be worth taking some risks.

Or was she just setting herself up for a huge heartbreak?

Days later, on Monday, Myra asked her to come visit and bring Hattie. When Talia told Nick, he arranged for a limo, which seemed ridiculous to Talia, but she didn't argue with him. She had stayed out of his bedroom Sunday night and they'd had the brothers over in the evening, so she hadn't been alone with him. Earlier that day they had all gone to church together and then taken Ida and Myra to a local restaurant in the closest small town to have Sunday dinner together. The brothers had come back to Nick's and all of them had disappeared into the barn until evening.

Even though Talia hadn't been alone with Nick since their wedding night, she was acutely aware of him, feeling the same sizzling fires when he touched her lightly or when they exchanged glances. More so now than ever before because they had made love and it had been scalding, raging hot sex that she thought about constantly when she was with him or not.

Monday night the brothers were back and Nick went with them to look at some of his horses in the barn again. Later on, when she went upstairs to put

Hattie to bed, she thought she was alone in the house. She had all the lights off except one, a small baby lamp with nursery-rhyme characters at the base. But in minutes Nick appeared. He knocked lightly on the door and came in.

"She's sound asleep, isn't she?"

"Yes," Talia said. "She had a big day. She's not used to all the attention, but she had a good time. She was good with your grandmother, sitting on her lap for as long as she did."

"You can't imagine how happy my grandmother is over Hattie. All of us are amazed. I don't remember that kind of joy with Artie, but Artie was so little and he wasn't talking."

"I'm glad. Hattie must sense that because she seems to really like your grandmother."

His fingers closed lightly on her arm. "Come here," he said softly and shivers tickled her. "She's asleep." They walked out of the bedroom into the sitting room and he turned to her. He reached up to take a lock of her hair in his hand and she felt the contact through her whole body, a touch that would be nothing if done by anyone else, but with Nick, it was electrifying.

"I can't control my dreams," he told her without preamble. "I was dreaming about Regina the other night but that didn't have anything to do with us."

"I know that, Nick. I thought we'd both sleep better if I came back here with Hattie. These are new surroundings. I want to be here for her if she wakes up. I understand and it didn't upset me," she said.

"Okay. I just didn't want to hurt you, but I can't control my dreams and I do dream about both of them. I haven't slept well since that plane crash."

"I'm sorry and I can imagine. You don't ever need to apologize where Regina and Artie are concerned. Not ever, not once. You had a devastating, terrible loss."

He looked away and was silent a moment. "Regina took him to see her folks in Montana. It was one of my planes, but not a small plane. It went down and all were killed. We had a pilot, copilot, Regina, her sister and Artie."

"I'm so sorry for your loss. Don't ever apologize for dreaming about them or anything like that. You loved them."

He drew her into his arms and she went eagerly. She slipped her arms around his waist and held him tightly, hoping she was some comfort, some company for him, and that Hattie would bring him love and joy.

"I'm going to sleep in here tonight, Nick. I'll feel better and I don't want to rush into a lusty physical relationship that we both might regret."

"I won't ever have a regret about making love with you. Oh, Talia, you can't imagine what you do to me," he whispered, trailing kisses on her throat and then running his tongue over the curve of her ear as he caressed her nape and sent waves of fiery tingles that centered low in her.

She drew a deep breath and wound her arms around his neck. "Nick, aren't your brothers here?"

"I guess. I left them in the barn." He shrugged. "But I don't care really. They know we just got married."

"Nick," she said, starting to protest when his lips covered hers, his tongue stroking hers so slowly while he caressed her breast. She gasped with pleasure and couldn't stop him or say anything else to him. She was hopelessly lost in sensations that made her yearn for his thick, hard manhood inside her.

"I wasn't going to do this tonight," she whispered, tearing her mouth away from his.

"Neither was I, but now we are and I don't want to stop." His mouth covered hers, his tongue going over hers while he pulled her zipper down her back and then peeled away her dress.

"Nick, we should use some sense here—"

"Shh," he whispered, unfastening her bra and letting it fall. His hands cupped her bare breasts and he stroked her so lightly, slowly, his thumbs circling her taut nipples, and then his mouth covered them so he could lave them with his tongue. She gasped and thrust her hips against him, grinding against him, wanting him inside her, forgetting all her lectures to avoid making love with him anytime soon. She was lost in his kisses and caresses. She trembled, gasping for air and moaning with pleasure as his hands moved over her and more of her clothing fell away.

"I wasn't going to do this," she whispered again, as if she could convince herself.

Nick didn't respond. He merely picked her up and carried her to his bedroom.

Before she could utter a protest, he assured her, "The monitor is on and we can hear Hattie."

Once in his bedroom, he stood Talia on her feet and peeled away the rest of her clothes, tossing his own aside as he kissed her.

She ran one hand through his hair and the other over his broad shoulder, down his back, over his hip and then over his butt that was hard and muscular like the rest of him. Against her, she felt his erection, thick and hard, ready for her. He picked her up and she locked her legs around his waist as he took her breast in his mouth and ran his tongue over her nipple.

She clung to him while he lowered her down over his body, sliding her onto his throbbing rod. She cried out and locked her legs around him, moving in perfect rhythm with him as he pumped into her. She cried out again as her climax burst and made her shake, relief and ecstasy showering over her. He thrust hard and fast toward his own climax.

In seconds or minutes—she didn't know time— she was aroused again, moving with him toward another shattering climax as she rode him.

When they were both sated, she had lost all track

of time. Finally she slid down and placed her feet on the floor. He looked into her eyes and she felt as if a bond sprang to life between them, a tie that bound them together in rapturous intimacy. She knew it couldn't last, but for a moment, she felt something from him beyond pure lust. He pulled her to him to kiss her, another earth-shaking kiss. His kiss set her on fire as if they hadn't just made love, as if she hadn't reached more than one explosive climax that still took her breath away to think about.

She leaned away a fraction, placing her mouth at his ear. "I wasn't going to do that. I was going to be sensible, cautious, and get to know you."

"Oh, what you do to me," he whispered, trailing his tongue lightly behind her ear. "You've brought me to life. Sensible went out the window with our first kiss. Life is filled with hurt. When we find fireworks and rapture, I say go for it."

"I have to agree. Life is filled with risks, Nick. We both took big ones with this loveless convenient marriage. We didn't factor in kisses and more."

"We didn't factor in the hottest sex ever. Talia, you should come with caution signs on you."

"I don't think it's me. I think it's *us*."

"If it's 'us' we've complicated our lives."

"I hope we haven't," she said.

He picked her up again to place her in his big bed and then stretch out beside her. He drew her close against him, tangling his long legs with hers.

Wrapped in euphoria, she held him while she ran

her hand lightly over his shoulders and chest, marveling at his strong, masculine body. "You know, I could stay like this with you forever. In your arms, touching you and—" She broke off and gasped.

He opened his eyes and looked at her. "What is it?"

She sat up like a bolt. "Your brothers! We're lying here...like this, and for all we know they could be somewhere in this house waiting for you to return."

He smiled and patted her shoulder in a gesture meant to calm her nerves. "Trust me, Talia, they're not here. They have that much sense. They've gone and locked up and forgotten about us." He glanced at the monitor on his nightstand. "And Hattie is asleep and I have you here, naked in my arms against my naked body, and I'm going to want to make love to you again."

He pulled her back down to him, and the instant she felt the heat of his chest, she felt herself relax. "I think I want you to do just that," she whispered, sliding sensuously against him. At her touch his body came to life and she began stroking his manhood. As if she hadn't found ecstasy in his arms twice already, she needed him again.

"Oh, yes, Nick," she said, sliding over him and sitting up astride him.

"You're a sex-starved woman," he said, but she knew it wasn't a complaint. Nick needed no coaxing to participate in another round of lovemaking.

With one hand he toyed with her breasts while the other stroked her inner thighs, up and down, each time venturing closer to the apex of her womanhood but never giving her the satisfaction she craved. She undulated her lips, giving him access, letting her body tell him what it wanted, needed.

Gently he pushed her down so his thick erection was between her legs, hot and hard, and he shifted his thighs, closing her legs against him. She gasped with need and moved against him, rubbing against him, relishing the silky smooth feel of him as she heightened his pleasure. But it wasn't enough. She wanted him inside her until she cried out with a mind-blowing climax.

Taking the matter into her own hands, she led him where she wanted him. Nick needed no further instructions. In one fluid motion he entered her to the hilt, eliciting a long moan from deep in her throat. Then he thrust into her, and she rode him hard and fast, until she didn't think she could take another second of this insane pleasure. With one final movement, they both climaxed at the same second, and letting out a sigh, she collapsed on him.

He wrapped his arms around her and she lay against him, relishing the feel of him still inside her. She didn't think she'd ever felt so comfortable. She'd certainly never felt so satisfied. Burrowing her head against his chest, she gave herself over to the feeling of utter contentment.

* * *

Her eyes flew open and were captured by the only light in the room. His alarm clock. It was almost four in the morning and they had made wild, passionate love all through the night. She'd lost count of how many times but she'd loved each and every one of them.

And what about the man who'd taken her to those heights?

She looked over at Nick, sleeping beside her. How deep did her feelings run for him now? She couldn't say. All she knew was that each day together, each moment of lovemaking, was stealing her heart away. There in the darkness of his bedroom she finally admitted what she'd feared all along. Despite her caution, despite the warning, there was no way she was going to be able to resist falling in love with Nick Duncan.

She'd always be grateful that he had given her the chance to become Hattie's mother, and for that reason she was glad she'd married him. But in securing Hattie as her daughter, she'd set something else at risk. Her heart.

Nick stirred and his arms blindly reached out for her. She went into them and knew she was in big trouble.

For the second day that week, Nick's grandmother had invited Talia to bring over Hattie for a visit. Once again, she found herself in Myra's smaller ranch house, sipping coffee while Hattie played on the floor and Myra joined in.

She couldn't help but think the older woman seemed to become more animated and kind whenever she was in Hattie's presence. And Hattie, too, seemed to enjoy playing with her great-grandmother.

"I've been thinking, Myra," Talia said. "Would you mind if I painted a picture of you with Hattie? I like to do portraits and I think it would be fun to have one of the two of you."

With a little doll in hand, Myra looked up. "That's fine with me. I'd like it, but I don't see how you can get Hattie to sit for a portrait."

Talia smiled. "I don't expect her to sit for the painting. I'd take a picture and then paint from that. I do it a lot of the time. She'll have to be still only a few seconds while I take her picture and she's accustomed to doing that." Talia couldn't count the number of Hattie photos stored on her phone.

"I'd love that," Myra said, smiling and glancing back down at Hattie, who was busy with a small dollhouse and a set of tiny dolls. "Can you dress her the same way she was for your wedding? She looked adorable."

"Actually, I have a good picture of the two of you from the party. Here, let me show you," she said, scrolling through her phone till she found the shot she was looking for. She showed Myra.

"Ahh, I like that one." In the picture Hattie was

sitting on Myra's lap and they were both smiling at the camera. Hattie had her pink bunny in her hands.

"Then I'll do a portrait of this. It'll be fun."

"I can't wait to see the result," Myra replied. Then she looked up at Talia. "You know, I've enjoyed having you here on the ranch. Both of you. I have a feeling now that you're here, I'll probably get to see Nick a lot more, too."

Hattie pulled herself up and stood holding on to Myra's leg. She gave a little giggle as she took the doll the older woman was holding.

"You're a beautiful little girl, Hattie," Myra said as she leaned over to kiss Hattie's cheek. "I had to wait a long time for another grandchild, but I couldn't ask for a more delightful one."

Talia knew all her concerns were unfounded. She needn't worry that Nick's family wouldn't accept and love Hattie. It was right in front of her eyes.

Myra sat up and looked at her. "You know, Talia, I'll be the first to admit I wasn't in accord with this wedding. But now I am so happy that you and Nick married. You're good for him and Hattie is a joy. You and Hattie are erasing his grief and for that I'm so thankful."

Talia felt a surge of love for Nick's grandmother. Another of her concerns went by the wayside. It seemed the Duncan family matriarch had accepted her, as well.

"Thank you, Myra. Nick has made it possible for

me to be Hattie's mother and for that I will forever be grateful to him."

"Just be patient with him. You and Hattie are going to take away his hurt."

That was the one thing she was still worried about. That Nick still hurt over his late wife and son. She'd never be able to erase his pain fully but maybe one day she could make it more bearable.

She reached over and patted Myra's hand. "I hope so."

Her hands were shaking.

As she twisted her hair and fastened it with a clip at the back of her head, she could barely keep her fingers from trembling. She smoothed down the navy suit and white silk blouse she'd chosen to wear and gave herself a final once-over in the gilded mirror of her suite in Dallas.

She could hardly believe this day had finally come. She was scared and eager at the same time to go to court for the adoption hearing. Taking a big deep breath, she left her room and went to pick up Hattie.

She'd dressed Hattie as she had been for the wedding, in her best dress. The little girl had no idea what was happening, the importance of this day. Talia figured it was just as well.

She carried Hattie downstairs to the library to meet Nick and Stan. Nick's brother had come to Dallas with them to help with Hattie while Talia and Nick were in court. Both men wore charcoal suits and black boots and hats. Stan's was Western style and he wore a bolo, while Nick's was a classic cut with a red tie. Stan was a handsome cowboy, but it was Nick who took her breath away. Just looking at him made her weak in the knees, made her think of the incredible pleasure he'd given her night after night.

But today she had other thoughts when she walked into the library and saw him. Today all she could think about was that he had made this moment possible. If all went well, she would be Hattie's legal mother by noon.

She walked to them, greeting Stan, who took Hattie from her and walked away to give her a moment with Nick.

"You look gorgeous," Nick said. "I'm sure the judge will take one look at you and give you whatever you want." He glanced down at his slim black watch. "We're right on time. Horace said he'll meet us at the courthouse and he said this won't take long." His hand at the small of her back urged her out the door, but she couldn't move.

"Nick, I am so scared."

"Don't be. Horace said everything will be fine. Believe me, he would know. Let's go get this done and you can relax and be happy," he said as he took her hands in his and led her to the car.

She felt as if she was in a daze when they walked into the empty courtroom with Nick's attorney. Stan sat on a front-row seat with Hattie with some toys in his pockets for her. Talia's nerves were prickly and she tried to breathe deeply and be calm. She glanced at Hattie, who sat looking at Stan's bolo and was quiet as if she, too, sensed this was a monumental moment in her life.

Looking official in his black robe, the judge appeared. Dazed, she went through questions she had to answer, listened as Nick answered questions. Fear enveloped her and she hoped she appeared calm. She told how she had known Hattie and how much care she had given her, how close she had been with Madeline, Hattie's mother. In addition, she had printed out all the pictures of her with Hattie and Madeline from her phone and iPad. The pictures started the day Hattie was born and chronicled her life until now, visible proof of Talia's presence and friendship with Madeline.

At one point Judge Wentworth wanted Hattie brought forward and Stan gave her to Talia. To her relief, Hattie was on her best behavior as she often was in new surroundings, and Judge Wentworth relaxed and smiled for the first time. When he spoke to Hattie, she turned to hug Talia and Talia held her close, glad Hattie had hugged her. She smiled at Judge Wentworth.

Time stretched, seeming endless, and Talia's nerves remained on edge. Shortly, she handed Hattie back to Stan while she and Nick signed papers.

She had no idea how much time passed until she officially became Hattie's mother.

"Congratulations. You have a beautiful daughter," Judge Wentworth said when it was official.

Talia felt giddy with happiness. She looked at the official document in her hand, and tears of joy and relief stung her eyes as she smiled and looked at Nick. She hugged him.

"Thank you," she whispered in his ear.

He hugged her lightly in return, and when she stepped back, he smiled. "Thank you, Talia. She needs you." Nick's attorney congratulated her and gave her best wishes before doing the same to Nick.

She couldn't keep back tears of relief and joy as Stan came up with Hattie to congratulate her. Hastily wiping away her tears, she took Hattie into her arms and hugged her.

"I love you, my precious baby. You're my baby now," she whispered to Hattie, not even knowing if Hattie heard her or understood her. Hattie wiggled and Stan took her again. As soon as he did, Nick hugged Talia.

Tears came again while she held him. "Nick, thank you. I'll be forever grateful to you."

"You've always loved her like she's your child. Now I'm glad she's your child by law. We'll all be better off. This is what I wanted when I proposed this marriage of convenience. Hattie needs your love."

She looked at Stan holding Hattie and pointing

to something out the window as he talked to her. She realized that when he was around Stan gave more attention to Hattie than Nick did, and she wondered when Nick would really treat her as his little girl.

Her gaze shifted to Hattie and joy made her smile. Hattie was really her daughter now. Nothing could mar the happiness she felt today.

She had another week lined up in Dallas. She needed to select wallpaper and decor for Hattie's rooms, as well as select the rest of the furniture for Hattie's nurseries in both Dallas and the ranch. Nick had said he would make arrangements for the contractor to get the work done on the suites. Whenever she had time and wanted to deal with it, she could make decisions about what she wanted for her art studio. Nick insisted she have a studio in Dallas as well as on the ranch, so she would. Nick's contractor would work on that, too, once he had Talia's input. That was something on her to-do list for this week.

She'd be in Dallas this week and Nick would be on the ranch. It was just as well that they were apart. It'd give them a chance to adjust to this new life they had. Sex was fantastic, but making love to Nick also meant she was becoming more emotionally involved with him. If they had too big an emotional conflict, it could hurt Hattie. And that was something she could never do.

* * *

At the end of the week, Nick waited on the porch for Talia and Hattie to get back from Dallas. He had on fresh jeans and a white cotton shirt that was open at the throat. He had missed them both—a surprise because he didn't think they had been in his life long enough to miss them at all. If he was truthful with himself, he'd admit that he missed Talia constantly, and he especially missed her at night. Their lovemaking had stunned him. She was hot, sexy, amazing in bed, though she'd given no indication of being that way until they were alone and began to touch and kiss. She had brought him back to life with an overwhelming burst of lust. At the oddest times throughout the day he was bowled over by thoughts of her, by the need to have her right there and then, naked in his bed.

After the loss of Regina and Artie, he had thrown himself into ranch work, which he had always enjoyed. He'd worked late and then gone home to take care of paperwork regarding the ranch. Beyond being a board member, he wasn't active any longer in the family energy company in Dallas. Since marrying Talia, though, he had started work earlier and, whenever possible, cut out some of the late-night work. On those unavoidable late nights when he missed dinner with her, she would come join him and he looked forward to having her there, to just being with her. He didn't know what it meant, but Talia seemed to draw him to her, like a magnet.

Something else was strange. In the time since she'd been in his life, his dreams had diminished. Those horrible nightmares that made him wake up in a sweat and in pain over losing his wife and baby.

He paced the porch and looked down at his watch. Where were they?

All week he'd been counting the hours until tonight. He had missed her enough to be shocked at how important she had become in his life. Along with that, he felt nagging twinges of guilt, because he still loved Regina and Artie. He tried to reassure himself that Regina would want him to go on with his life, but that didn't assuage the guilt. In fact, it increased the more he was drawn to Talia. In some ways it was difficult for him to relate to a little girl, but Talia made up for any lack of love from him because she poured out her love on Hattie. So did his grandmother and brothers.

He squinted down the road, looking for any sign of kicked-up dust that would signal her arrival. Damn. He wished she'd get back soon. He'd carry her off to bed the minute she arrived.

Each day she'd been away they had talked several times and for more than an hour each time. The text messages had flown back and forth, too. But it wasn't the same as having her beside him. And Hattie, too.

He drew a deep breath when the limo finally appeared. Nick was down the steps, running to meet them, when Talia stepped out. She wore a maroon dress that ended just above her knees, leaving her long, shapely legs bare. She unbuckled Hattie and then turned around to face him.

He hugged her lightly, catching a whiff of some exotic perfume, surprising himself again how glad he was they were home.

When he picked up Hattie to hug her, she put her slender little arm around his neck to hug him. She leaned away. "Wuv you," she said, smiling at him, and Nick felt a clinch to his heart.

"Oh, sweet baby, I love you," he said, feeling a knot in his throat as he looked into green eyes so like his own, only on a sweet little face that made him weak in the knees. It still hurt to know he would never hear Artie say those words to him, but he was hearing his little daughter say them.

"I'm glad you're both back," he said. "I have presents for you," he said to Hattie.

She giggled up at him and ran her chubby little hands across his cheeks.

"Let's go see what your presents are," he said and reached out to drape his arm across Talia's shoulders. "Hi."

"Hi, Nick," she said, smiling at him. The moment he looked into her eyes, he felt sparks fly between them. He couldn't understand the chemistry between them. All he knew was that it took his breath away and, as usual, made him want to rush her off to the bedroom as soon as possible.

"I couldn't keep from getting emotional over that

greeting. It's a reminder I won't ever hear Artie say those words to me."

"No, but you are hearing Hattie say them to you. If you let her, she'll wrap herself around your heart and put it in her collection. She's a sweetie."

"I'm glad you two are back at the ranch and so is the rest of the family. Stan wants us all for Sunday dinner. Grandmother can't wait to see Hattie and I promised you two would come over today after you got in."

"That's good. I'll be happy to see her."

"I have all sorts of plans for later," he said, looking into her blue eyes that held his gaze.

"So do I," she said and his pulse raced.

They went to the family room and he picked up a box wrapped in red paper. Another present in blue paper was beside it.

"Here, Hattie, this is a present for you," Nick said, handing it to her.

She smiled and began to try to tear off the wrapping. She yanked free the stick-on bow and tossed it behind her. When she couldn't open the box, Nick helped.

"Dolly," she squealed, picking up a fancy doll with long blond hair and a pink satin dress. She hugged it to her chest.

"Thank you," Talia said to Nick, slowly and clearly so Hattie would hear and begin to learn the words. Hattie smiled at him and hugged her doll.

Nick watched her, happy because she was happy.

Then he turned to Talia and took her hand, feeling her smooth, soft skin and wanting to run his hands all over her and lose himself in her softness. "Thank you for bringing her into my life. I could have so easily never known about her."

They exchanged a look and he didn't know exactly what she was thinking, but he suspected she was thinking how close she, too, had come to losing Hattie.

He shifted closer to put his arm around Talia as they watched Hattie. Nick gave his daughter the next present, which was a book that she immediately wanted Talia to read to her.

As he watched them huddle together as Talia read the story, Nick had only one thought: life was good.

It was almost nine by the time they put Hattie to bed. When they left Hattie's room, Nick took Talia's hand.

"Come here," he said.

"Nick—"

"Shh. Come with me," he said, leading her to his suite, where a lamp was turned low. "Hattie isn't the only one getting a present," he said, holding out a box wrapped in white paper and tied with a blue satin bow. She looked up at him with wide eyes.

"Mine? Are you aware this is June, not December? Why the presents, Nick?"

"I have presents for Hattie because she's my little girl. And presents for you because you're my wife now and you've been patient, understanding and kind. You got a raw deal in some ways even though you got what you wanted—Hattie. Anyway, here's a little token of my thanks."

She stepped close and put her arm around his neck, pulling him closer as she brushed a light kiss on his mouth. Her lips were velvety soft, pure temptation.

"I didn't get a raw deal," she whispered. "I'm so happy, Nick. I've told you, that was my fantasy fulfilled, to get to keep her. You can't imagine how scared and worried I've been about Hattie, especially before I met you."

"Shh." His arm circled her waist. "That's all over. She's your daughter now and forever." He tightened his arm around her and really kissed her. It took only a startled second before she responded, her tongue meeting his, setting him ablaze. Then suddenly she pulled away.

"I have a present to open," she whispered, holding it up.

"I thought my kiss might make you forget the present," he teased and she smiled.

"I'll get back to you in a few minutes," she said in a sultry voice that made his pulse jump.

She untied the bow, tearing off the paper and opening the box. She gasped as the light caught the diamond pendant. "Nick, this pendant is absolutely gorgeous." She took it out of the box. "This is so beautiful. Put it on me, please," she said and turned so he could.

He lifted it over her head and fastened the catch, brushing light kisses on her nape as he did so. She turned to face him.

"It's so beautiful. Thank you," she said and kissed him again.

As they kissed, his hands went to her blouse to unbutton it. He wanted her with a hungry need so intense he was surprised.

"I'm so glad you're home," he whispered. He pushed her blouse off her shoulders. "You're beautiful, so gorgeous."

He picked her up and carried her to his bed, yanking away the covers again. "Let me show you how much I've missed you."

Talia clung to him, wanting him yet holding back the words that she wanted to say, words that would tell him how much she cared for him, how important he had become to her. But now was not the time. Not when he was doing things to her body that drove away all conscious thought.

She could only moan in pleasure and longing as heat spread low in her belly and desire made her pulse race. His hand caressed her breasts and she felt them tighten. In another second she wouldn't be able to stop the sexual onslaught. She was torn between desiring him and protecting her heart. She was dallying with trouble, with seduction and heartbreak, yet his scalding kisses were fanning flames that wiped out all her half-hearted arguments.

For a few minutes or a long time, she didn't know, she kissed him in return. She wanted his loving, wanted all of him, wanted his body against hers and wanted more nights of his kisses. She had made her decision to take the risks with Nick. Life was filled with risks and it was worth taking a risk with her new husband, who had been so marvelous to Hattie and to her. They had repeated marriage vows that she felt they each would live by and that meant they would be together, for a lifetime. Even as she thought about it, his hands, his lips were driving all rational thought out of mind while a tiny, nagging voice still whispered warnings of a broken heart. Emotionally, she was torn. Physically, she desired him more than ever. When his hand slid over the curve of her hip and found the part of her that ached for him, she knew she couldn't deny her body what it craved.

Emboldened, she unbuttoned and pushed away his clothes and in seconds he was naked before her. When she reached out for his erection, grasping it in her palm, she heard his sharp intake of breath even as her heart thudded.

"You are so beautiful," he whispered as he cupped her breasts, pausing to look at her before he leaned forward to run his tongue over her nipple, circling it slowly, his tongue warm and wet. She gasped with pleasure, closing her eyes and letting him loose in order to cling to his hard biceps. He ran his tongue over her ear, down on her throat, then down over her breast while his fingers worried both nipples, slowly, featherlight.

She moaned softly with pleasure and desire, needing more, aching for him.

"I want you," she whispered. "Now. Inside me. I've missed you."

"We won't rush. I want to pleasure you. I want to take our time," he whispered, showering kisses between his words—words she barely heard over the drumming of her heart. She pressed against him and leaned away a fraction to rub her breasts against him.

"Ahh, Talia, what you do to me," he whispered as he picked her up. He placed her on his bed and then knelt between her legs, running his hands so lightly over her inner thighs, his fingers brushing her intimately. When he followed with his tongue, sensations bombarded her, but she was even more aware of the handsome, naked man caressing her, kneeling between her legs.

She gasped with pleasure, arching beneath him. His tongue drove her wild, yet she didn't want to end it that way. Instead, she pushed him back and sat up to straddle his legs. She leaned down and ran her tongue down his chest as her fingers danced over him.

"You have to be the sexiest man on this earth," she whispered and then ran the tip of her tongue beside the path of hair that arrowed to his impressive erection. She moved down, trailing wet kisses up his shaft, but when she opened her mouth to take him in, he stopped her. He grabbed her in his big hands and in a flash he was over her and she was beneath him and he was filling her as she arched to meet him.

Wrapping her long legs around him, she held him tightly. She cried out, raising her hips while he thrust slowly, taking time to heighten every pleasure, to build her needs.

When she lost control, she moved with him, both together as they strained to reach a pinnacle. His thick rod filled her, sensations rocking her. She cried out with release, her legs tight around him while she clung to him.

His release burst, spilling hotly inside her, giving her what she sought. Gasping for breath, she held him as he clung to her and they moved together, causing more waves of pleasure to pour over her.

His arms tightened around her, solid, reassuring as they pumped together and shared the moment. With a cry, ecstasy rippled through her when she climaxed again. Finally she was still, gasping for breath as much as he was.

He brushed long, damp strands of silken hair away from her face and caressed her cheek so lightly. "That had to be the sexiest climax I've ever reached," he said, looking down at her. "You're fantastic."

And so was he, she thought. And that was the problem. "Nick, we can't do this every night."

He shook his head and looked at her, as if he didn't believe what he heard. "We can't? Why not?"

"Because one of us might fall in love and the other one would not."

Her words obviously had no effect on him, because he didn't move off her. "I don't want this night to end. I want to kiss and touch and explore and hug straight through the weekend. Promise me you won't get out of bed or out of my arms."

"I'm afraid you're not getting that promise, but I'm here now." His body was hot, hard, muscled and masculine. As much as she shouldn't, she wanted nothing else but to run her fingers over him, discover every inch of him, memorize his body and everything about him that she could learn about him.

"Stay here with me tonight. I want you here in my arms. I want you close to me," he said, leaning down to kiss her tenderly. Then he turned, keeping her with him.

She slept with his arm around her. At one point during the night she turned to watch him as he slept and knew she was in love with him. It was too late to avoid that now.

She couldn't see him as an ordinary person. When he was around, she was excited, continually aware of him, still getting streaks of fire from the slightest physical contact with him. She was falling more in love with him with each day she spent around him. And it was likely he would never be in love with her.

* * *

On the Fourth of July, Nick and his brothers had a cookout on the ranch. All hands, their families, neighbors and friends were invited. Talia found it amazing how well and smoothly the day went. She watched with other moms while Hattie played with some of the little kids who lived on the ranch, but her favorite part of the day was when Nick had Hattie on his broad shoulders and her fingers were wound in his thick hair while she laughed. Talia wished Nick would spend more time like this with Hattie. She knew they both needed to make adjustments and they would, but he was still working too late lots of nights, coming in too late to see Hattie. He knew she poured love out to Hattie and he seemed to feel that was sufficient, but Talia wanted Hattie to have Nick's love, his attention. Whenever she worried about how little he saw his daughter, she reminded herself that he probably needed more time to adjust.

As she watched him play, she thought about being with him later and excitement streaked through her like a lightning bolt, burning up all her concerns.

The rest of the week, Talia spent most of her time getting her art studio set up and checking on the progress of the nursery. She worked some on the portrait of Myra and Hattie together. Friday night Nick came in early. He cooked out and they ate on the patio. Afterward, they drove to his grandmother's house to visit for a short time because she loved to see Hattie.

It was after one in the morning by the time Nick and Talia were in bed with Talia pressed against his side. He had his arm around her and she felt content, satiated, so happy after the day and night.

"Nick, I loved it that you came in early enough tonight for the three of us to eat together like a family and to give you time to play with Hattie."

"I liked it, too. I'll try to get in earlier more often. There are always things to do."

"There's a little girl who needs your love."

"She has that. You pour love out to her all day. She isn't going to lack for love. Neither are you," he said, turning to kiss her.

"Are you getting love mixed up with sex?"

"Is that a complaint?" he asked and she could hear the amusement in his voice.

"Absolutely not. I have no complaints," she said, knowing she would never admit to him that she often wished he showed more affection for Hattie.

Later, as she lay in his arms, she ran her fingers over his shoulder. "I need to get up and get my nightgown," she said, running her fingers over the stubble on his jaw. "You sexy man. And, oh, what muscles you have," she said, running her hand over his biceps and then across his shoulders and on his chest. "Oh, my."

"You keep that up and you'll start something again."

"Let me try and see if I can," she said, smiling at him. "I think I was going to get a nightgown."

"You definitely don't need one. I like you naked. You're warm and soft. I might wake and want to hold you. I don't want anything in the way."

She smiled at him. "I suspect you can get me out of that nightgown very quickly."

Before he could answer her, his phone rang.

"It's almost two in the morning—damn late for a phone call. This isn't going to be good news." He retrieved his phone and looked at it and frowned, and she hoped it wasn't terrible news.

He sat up in bed. "This is Nick." He was quiet for a moment and then he drew a deep breath. "Oh, damn. I'll be there. I'll call Stan now. I'll talk to my brothers."

She let her fingers drift lazily over his bare back. "Go ahead," he said into the phone, but she noticed his voice had changed, gotten deeper. Chills broke out over her arms and she slipped out of bed to grab the nearest piece of clothing. She wrapped his white shirt around her, suddenly so cold.

Eight

"I'll see you in about twenty minutes," he said right before he ended the call. Talia knew what that meant. Twenty minutes meant something had happened on the ranch. He couldn't get off the ranch and get somewhere else in twenty minutes.

He gulped deep breaths and suddenly threw his phone across the room, where it hit a chair and bounced onto the floor with a clatter.

"What's happened?" she asked, knowing it was really bad news.

"I have to go. I have to call my brothers first." But he didn't move. He sat at the side of the bed, his head down.

She waited quietly, giving him space, knowing he would talk to her when he was ready.

"My grandmother died tonight," he said softly without even moving. "She went to sleep and…died. She just quit breathing. Ida said she never heard a sound from her."

"Oh, Nick," Talia said, feeling a gut-wrenching pain inside. "I'm so sorry that's happened."

"When Ida went in to check on her, she realized Grandmother wasn't breathing. They called an ambulance and it should be here any minute now."

He turned to look at her then and his face was tight, his eyes dark. More than anything she wanted to reach out for him, but his posture told her to stay away.

"Just when she had something to live for and she was happy, filled with enthusiasm and energy to get to know Hattie. She loved Hattie and Hattie seems to have loved her. I wanted Hattie to know her." His eyes filled with tears and he wiped them with his fingers. "There's too much death in my life. Too damn many losses. We were all so happy. She was happy again. We haven't seen her like this in years." He slammed the mattress beside him and stood up. "Dammit to hell. One more death instead of life and joy."

Talia knew there wasn't anything she could say or do that would help him. She could just be there for him.

"I have to call my brothers and I want to go over

there before they take her body to the funeral home. I'll probably have to call the sheriff since she died unexpectedly at home. I don't know. They'll tell me when the ambulance arrives."

"Can I do anything?" she asked quietly.

"Just watch Hattie." He got out of bed, yanked on his briefs and jeans before picking up his phone.

Talia quietly gathered her clothes that had been tossed in haste only a short while ago.

"Poor Hattie." He sighed as he pocketed his phone. "She lost her mother and now her grand-mother. At least she has the two of us. Today she has us. Who knows who she'll have in a month?" He ground out the words and she knew he was hurting.

"I'll get dressed, Nick," she said, leaving him, feeling she couldn't comfort him and that he prob-ably wanted to be alone.

She showered quickly and dressed. Then she crossed the bedroom to look in on Hattie. The little girl was on her side, holding her new doll. Her pink bunny was on her other side.

Talia went back to find Nick. He was on the phone with one of his brothers.

"I'll see you there, Blake. I'll call Mr. Morton at the funeral home."

She stood in the doorway, listening to him make his calls. Finally, he looked up and saw her. "I've talked to my brothers, also to the officials. I'll go over to Grandmother's now. Thanks for staying with Hattie."

"I live here, Nick." She crossed the room to him. "I'm sorry for your loss."

"Yeah, well, thanks. It's just too many, Talia. I feel like ripping my heart out and never loving again because it hurts to keep losing people I love. It hurts a damn lot. You might be a lot safer if you'd just stay the hell away from me."

She felt as if an invisible wall of anger surrounded him and shut her away. If he shut her away, he would Hattie, too.

"I'm here if you want me."

He drew her to him, pulling her down on his lap to hug her, sitting quietly holding her. "She was just so damn happy with Hattie and Hattie liked her. They would have had fun together," he said.

"Yes, they would have," she replied, stroking the back of his head. "At least, Nick, they got to know each other. Your grandmother got to give Hattie things that she wanted Hattie to have. We'll have pictures of them together to give Hattie and tell her about her great-grandmother."

"I'm glad, but that was too little, too late. There are too many losses, too many hurts. This just does it for me. I don't want to love another person because I lose them. I have to go. I'll talk to you tomorrow. You go on to bed."

"You know I'm not going to sleep. Go to your grandmother's. If you want me to come with you I can take Hattie. She'll sleep."

"No. There's no need in dragging you and Hattie

over there, and if Hattie wakes, she'll just look for Grandmother. Aw, dammit." He ran a hand through his tousled hair. "She was bossy and gave me a hard time growing up, but I loved the old girl and I had to admire her because she was a strong woman. If my dad was drinking when we were growing up, she'd run him off." Nick shifted and Talia stood so he could get up.

"I better go," he said. "This is going to be a long night. Don't wait up. Tomorrow I'll get with my brothers and our pastor and we'll plan a service."

"I won't be asleep when you get back, so don't worry about waking me. If you want me, come to my room."

"Don't wait up for me. I might stay over there the rest of tonight with my brothers," he said as he picked up his wallet and keys from his dresser and turned to leave. Then he stopped and looked at her. "Somehow it's impossible to imagine life without her in it. She's been around the most and lasted the longest of any relative I've had."

Then he simply slipped out the door.

Four days later Nick stood by a window in the library on the ranch. They had their own cemetery and the grave had been opened and was ready for his grandmother's casket later today. He hurt and this loss brought back too many memories of the deaths of Regina and Arthur. He meant what he had told Talia. He intended to guard his heart, to keep from

loving one more person because it hurt too badly
to keep losing those he loved. He didn't want to get
any closer to Hattie and Talia. Not at this point in
his life. He and Talia were committed to a marriage
of convenience, but love had never been part of the
deal. And he intended to keep it that way.

He thought of the nights he'd spent making love
with Talia. The sexiest nights he'd ever had. They
could still have that. Love hadn't been part of it and
no words of love had ever been uttered by either one
of them. He just needed to keep love out of it.

What about Hattie? That little charmer could
steal his heart away and make him as vulnerable to
hurt as he had been over Arthur. That little son of
his, who couldn't even talk, had wrapped around his
heart. He had loved Artie so much. He could still
shed tears over him and he felt he would the rest of
his life. The same with Regina.

He wasn't going to give his heart to one more person, big or little. Today he better just worry about
getting through the ceremony and the graveside service and then he could think clearly about those
close to him in his life. Talia and Hattie. His heart
would be hostage to them if he let go and loved
them.

He heard voices and high heels and turned. His
breath caught when Talia came through the door.
She wore a black sleeveless dress with a straight
skirt that ended just below her knees. She was in
high-heeled black pumps. Her hair was fastened in

a bun at the back of her head. She wore very little makeup and she looked gorgeous.

He missed her. Over the last few days they had avoided each other, and he hadn't seen much of Hattie, either. She was in Talia's arms, and when she saw him, she held out her hands and Nick took her. She smiled at him, running her small fingers over his jaw.

His eyes met Talia's. "You look beautiful, even today."

"Thank you," Talia said.

"If she were here, my grandmother would give me a lecture. She'd tell me to be thankful I have you in my life."

Gently she put her hand on his shoulder. "You're going through a bad time, Nick. You're tough and you'll get through it and then life will settle back more like it was."

He just started walking to the door. "Let's go get this service over with."

The service was held in the closest small town, and then the family and friends went back for the burial in the cemetery on the ranch where Nick's grandfather, great-grandparents, an aunt and an uncle and two cousins, his mother, his first wife and his baby boy were buried. The minister spoke and then the service was over and people filed by to give Nick and the rest of his family condolences.

Talia moved out of the way with Hattie and finally they got back in the limos to go to Nick's house for the repast. It seemed forever till everyone ate, shared memories of Myra and went on their way. Finally, long after Hattie had been put to bed, Nick's brothers left.

Nick closed the door and faced her. "Thanks, again, for being a help. Just being here. You and Hattie were bits of cheer in an otherwise hellish day."

She nodded in acknowledgment. "It was a nice service. Your relatives and Myra's friends all spoke so highly of her."

"You'll finish Grandmother's picture with Hattie, won't you?"

"Of course."

"I stopped in your studio and looked at it. It's good. I wish she could see it because it would have really pleased her. Talia, today has been another day of pain and loss. But I want to forget it now, to kiss and make love and feel alive." He embraced her and leaned down to kiss her, his tongue claiming hers as he held her tightly. In seconds, desperate need rose up in him and he picked her up and strode to his bedroom.

As soon as he stood her on her feet, he peeled away her black dress, running his hands over her silken skin, feeling her softness against him, wanting her with all his being. He wanted to lose himself in hot sex that drove the world away. And he could do that with her. He paused to look at her and she opened her eyes. Her lips were parted from his kiss. "You're beautiful and you're the sexiest woman

I've ever known. I want all I can get of you tonight because you drive away my demons and make me feel alive."

"I want to make you feel that life is good because it is, Nick. You have to take some risks and we all get hurt, but life is good."

"Sex with you is what's good—more than good. I want you now."

Nick took her in his arms and kissed her hard, and she met his need with a passion of her own.

Unlike their other nights together, this time their lovemaking was fast. Talia let him set the pace, knowing what he needed tonight.

He shed his clothes and met her on the bed, already sheathed in protection. He moved between her legs, and as he claimed her mouth, he entered her. She wrapped her long legs around him and moved with him, holding him tightly, meeting his thrusts with her own. His hands were on her, touch making her want more, driving her closer to orgasm as she arched against him. With a hard thrust he sent her over the edge and she climaxed in a burst of ecstasy. Still, he pumped wildly, exciting her again, and in minutes she reached a second climax while he shuddered with his.

"Ahh, Nick, I love you."

The words were out. They were spoken in the throes of an orgasm that enveloped her in rapture and sensuous pleasure. But she couldn't take them back. Nor did she want to.

Dimly, she was aware that he hadn't made any responding declaration of love, but that thought was swiftly gone as she relished her spectacular sexual release.

He pulled her close in his arms. Their hot bodies were damp, legs tangled, arms holding each other while he showered light kisses on her and combed her hair away from her face. "You're beautiful, Talia. Fantastic to make love to," he whispered. "I want you in my bed every night."

That was as close to a declaration of love as she was going to get, she told herself. Not that she expected one, especially tonight.

Nick fell asleep quickly in her arms, and as she gazed into the darkness, she told herself that she had no one else to blame but herself. She'd cautioned herself to guard her heart, warned herself that he had a steel wall around him. But she hadn't heeded the warnings. She'd fallen in love...but Nick only wanted sex. She wanted to share her life, but he only wanted to share his bed.

She'd gone and done the unthinkable. Now could she settle for what he offered and be happy?

Nick woke and felt the empty bed. Talia had gone to her room sometime during the night. Before, she stayed in bed with him until they both got up. What he missed was seeing Hattie. He had gotten into the habit of tiptoeing in to look at her as she slept. She was never awake when he got up and left, so he would stand at her crib and look at her, amazed she was his little girl, thinking every morning how precious she was. He had stopped going in to see her. He hurt, and loving Talia and Hattie just made his heart a hostage. Hattie hadn't known he came in to see her in the mornings, so she wouldn't miss him now that he had stopped.

Sometimes he couldn't keep from thinking all through the day about Talia and their passionate, wild lovemaking, which made him long to go home and be with her.

At night he kept busy so he didn't come home until late. He wasn't going to get closer with Talia and Hattie. He had had so much pain and loss, he just wanted to get over the hurt and then pick up with life. Someday he might risk his heart again, but not yet. He'd heard Talia declare her love, but she had been in the throes of sex. He didn't think she was in love with him. After all, they had gone into this marriage knowing they weren't in love.

He wondered if he would lose Talia because of his lack of attention during the day. He hoped not. But he didn't think he would lose her because she needed him to be a father to Hattie.

Besides, they had their nights together.

Talia could no more resist making love with him than he could resist her. When he crawled into her bed late at night or picked her up and carried her to his room, he could kiss away any slight hesitation.

He had gone over and over everything in his mind and he always came up with the same answers. For a time, he intended to guard his heart from another terrible hurt. Hattie wouldn't miss him and he and Talia still had hot, sexy nights of passion that made them both forget everything else. Would he ever be able to let go again and love someone without fearing he would lose them, too?

Talia missed Nick—the Nick she had known before his grandmother's demise. Since then, Nick had thrown himself into work, leaving before dawn in the mornings and not getting in until late at night. When he wanted sex, he would pick her up from her bed to take her to his, kissing her the moment she stirred and started to speak to him. Any protest she had was gone the moment his mouth, his lips, his tongue were on hers.

During the day she lectured herself because their relationship wasn't what she wanted and he was avoiding Hattie and that hurt. But at night when he carried her to his bed, she would melt in his arms, all her arguments she had rehearsed blown to oblivion. She couldn't resist him, and sex was as fiery and spectacular as ever.

It was the second week of August when Nick came in at half past ten and found Talia sitting and waiting for him. He hadn't seen her for over a week and his first impression was she looked more gorgeous than he remembered. Her blond hair spilled in spiral curls around her face. She wore a plain blue cotton blouse with the first buttons unfastened, revealing the beginnings of full, soft curves and creamy skin, and he remembered exactly how it felt to fill his hands with her soft breasts.

"You're usually not up this late," he said. "I haven't seen you like this. You look great."

"No, you haven't seen me and thank you for the compliment. I'm not sure Hattie will know you now. You rarely see her, either, Nick. You really aren't a daddy to her any longer," she said softly.

"I pay her bills and I know you'll take care of her," he said.

Guilt filled him for avoiding them, but then he thought again about the losses in his life when he'd loved someone. "I'll come home earlier tomorrow and spend some time with her." He knew that was what he should do.

"We won't be here," she said coolly. "I'm taking her to Dallas for a few weeks."

Her words were like a knife to his gut.

He looked hurt, but she steeled herself. "I'll get a condo there," she told him. She'd already reached out to a Realtor she knew in the city.

"You don't need to get a condo. You can stay at my house. You can stay at a hotel and charge it to me if you want." He crossed the room to her, then reached down and pulled her to her feet. "Don't go, Talia. I want you here. Both of you. Nights with you are the best. They're special and keep me going."

"Nick, this isn't any way to live," she said, aware of his warm hands holding hers, of how close he stood. Every touch was sexy and made her want his kisses, but she couldn't live on sex alone. Outside of the bedroom he was moving out of her life. He had already gone out of Hattie's and that was what she couldn't take. She couldn't risk Hattie getting hurt.

"Nick, when we decided on this marriage of convenience, I knew what I was getting into because you were clear that you were not in love with me, but you said you would love and be a dad for Hattie. You're not being a daddy to her. You avoid her."

"I will be a dad to her. I can come home earlier and be with you and Hattie. I'll do that tomorrow night."

"I don't want just one night and then you're gone again for the next few weeks. I know you hurt badly over Regina, over Arthur, over Myra. But loss is a part of life. You've shut yourself off from life, from Hattie. Hattie no longer means anything to you."

"I feel if I give my love to anyone else, I'll lose them, too. I can't take any more loss. I can't just shut off all the heartaches I've had."

"No, I suppose you can't, but Hattie is out of your life. She's too precious for her to have that kind of father. I think for a little while we'll stay in Dallas and let you make some decisions about what you want and who you want in your life."

"I want the two of you. I thought I made that abundantly clear before you moved here." He placed his hand on her waist and his other hand slipped behind her neck to caress her nape lightly. She drew a deep breath and tried to keep on track, to avoid letting him touch and entice her until she forgot what she had planned to do.

"I don't want to keep on living this way, where she doesn't even see you. Nick, life is a risk, but most people think life is worth the risks. I do. You know what your grandmother would think about you withdrawing from Hattie. She'd tell you that's not living and it's not doing Hattie any good. She needs a daddy in her life who loves her and helps her. I know you've been generous financially, but she doesn't need your money. I'm able to take care of her without it. But it's your love she needs. The love, the living, the willingness to take some risks because you love someone enough to do so." She gazed into his stormy green eyes that had darkened with anger, but she didn't care. She wasn't going on this way and she wouldn't let him go on this way with Hattie.

"I'll take the limo to Dallas. I need to work out the future because I'm not coming back here to a life like this. I'll be gone when you get home tomorrow night, but you know where to find me. And I'm not going to your room tonight. Thank you for all you did, Nick. You gave me Hattie and I'll always be grateful for that, and for getting to know your family."

He lowered his hands from her and for a moment he said nothing. He just looked into her eyes. "Let me know if you want or need anything."

Then he stood up and walked away and she felt as if he were taking her heart with him. She thought about Hattie, peacefully sleeping in her little bed, blissfully unaware of the storm swirling around her and how her life would be rearranged again.

Talia gave Nick time to get to his room, then put her head in her hands and cried. She loved him and she knew he hurt, but this way of life wasn't doing any of them any good. Losing Myra had destroyed Nick but her loss was ironic. Because his strong grandmother would have been the first to tell Nick to pull himself together and go on with living.

Talia wiped away her tears. Go on with living. That was just what she had to do.

By the end of the following week her life had been transformed again. She'd had interviews with two local colleges to teach, and both looked like promising jobs when the next school year started. Talia had enough of her own money from her parents' insurance, and from her own savings, to care for Hattie without touching the funds Nick had provided. She used some to lease a condo near one of the colleges. She missed Nick and tried to keep busy so she wouldn't think about him, but everything reminded her of him. Nick was a forceful person and it was impossible to just forget him. She hurt and she missed him, and sometimes she was angry that he had shut himself off, especially from Hattie. The days were tough, but she busied herself with her daughter's care. But the nights… Nights were the worst when she wanted to be in his arms, wanted his kisses and his loving. Too many nights she cried herself to sleep, and at the same time, she hated that she couldn't forget him.

And then she missed a period.

Nick sat on his porch, trying to focus on the clock that he was trying to fix, but his thoughts kept wandering to the two females who were missing from his life. Talia and Hattie. He missed them constantly, especially in the evenings. Nights were hell, when he got into his big bed without Talia. And he missed Hattie's laughter, her little arms around his neck and her happy "Wuv you" declarations. He'd run them off by his total focus on his own pain and lost them just as much as he had lost Regina and Artie. Only this time it was due to his own stubbornness. Talia had hurt over the loss of his grandmother and then he had just hurt her more. And he hated to think he had hurt Hattie.

But what could he do?

He fumbled some more with the repair, but he couldn't reassemble the many clock pieces spread out on the table before him. It was kind of like his own life, he thought. All in pieces. Just as he probably wasn't going to get this clock working again, more than likely he wouldn't get his life in order, either.

He was miserable without Talia and Hattie. Really miserable. But what could he do?

He heard a motor and looked up from the repair to see Stan's pickup approaching. In minutes Stan stepped out of his truck and walked up on the porch. "Good morning, bro. What are you doing?"

"Trying to fix this old clock," Nick said.

"I have some things of Grandmother's that turned up in her attic. I brought them over for you and Talia to go through and see if you want anything for Hattie. They're in the truck."

"All right. Thanks. Set them on the table and I'll get them to her." He went back to work on the clock.

"Where's Hattie? I want to say hello. I haven't seen her for a couple of weeks now and that's way too long. She'll forget who I am."

With a long sigh, Nick pushed aside a screwdriver. "She's not here. She's in Dallas."

"Oh, okay. When will she be back? I'll come by. I've got a little toy for her. It's a windup kitty and it rolls around on the floor."

"That's nice, Stan. You'll have to go to Dallas to give it to her."

"How so?"

Nick looked up and saw his brother's eyes were

narrowed. "Talia left and took Hattie with her. End of story."

"The hell you say. What did you do?"

"Look, what I do with my wife is my business."

"This sort of touches all of us, Nick. You had to have run them off because two days before Grandmother's death, Talia told me how wonderful it was for Hattie to be in this family. And at that time Talia sounded happy to be part of this family, too. So tell me, what have you done?"

"You sound just like Grandmother, only I can tell you that it's none of your dang business."

"You ran Talia off. Why? We can find out from her, so you might as well tell me. And I will go see her."

Nick stood up and faced his brother. "Look, I'm tired of people I love dying on me. My wife died. My baby died. Grandmother died. I just don't want to get deeply involved with anyone right now and that includes Hattie and Talia."

"I'll be damned. You're scared of life, Nick." He took off his hat and ran a hand through his hair as he sat beside his brother. "This time your fear is going to cost you something really precious and special. When did you get this way?"

"When those I love died on me."

"That's part of life. Grandmother had a good life and she was eighty-seven years old. It hurts, but you pick up and go on and you don't shut off an adorable kid like Hattie or a woman like Talia. Where is she?"

"I don't even know. She's in Dallas, but I don't know where or doing what. All I know is she isn't staying in my house."

"I hope she isn't already dating someone, because if she isn't, she will be soon. In fact, I just may go see her and tell her to divorce you and marry me. I'd treat her right. In fact, when I tell them, Blake and Adam might go after her and tell her to pick one of us. We won't even let you come see her or Hattie. It would serve you right."

Stan stood up and rushed down the steps, taking them two at a time. "Have a nice life by yourself."

"Where are you going?"

"To Dallas, you jerk. Get ready for a divorce."

He glared at the back of his younger brother's head. "You wouldn't dare propose to her and she wouldn't accept," he called out.

Stan didn't turn around. He just shot over his shoulder, "But someone else will."

Nick glared at Stan as he jumped in his truck. The wheels spun and he left, stirring up dust and speeding away.

"Dammit." Nick shook his head. Stan was hot-headed enough to propose to his wife, but Nick had to believe Talia had sense enough to turn him down. But his brother was right. There just might be one guy she wouldn't turn down.

The thought of her divorcing him and marrying someone else hurt.

He looked at the pieces of clock spread all over

the table and knew what he had to do. He had to get his life back together.

He'd try calling her again, but she probably wouldn't answer, the same way she didn't take any of his dozens of calls before. He simply had to go find her.

The more he thought about it, the more he wanted her back. She was right. Life was filled with risks, but some of them were worth taking a chance on. He had hurt a whole lot more since she left and he wanted her back. He wanted his precious little girl back in his life. Because, as much as he hated to admit it, he loved his wife and daughter.

Talia glanced at her cell phone when a call came in. Nick had called more than a dozen times and twice today, but she didn't see any point in talking to him. She needed to make some decisions. She would have to talk to him someday, but she wasn't ready yet.

When her phone rang again, she glanced down at the screen and her stomach tightened when she saw it was a call from Stan. Something had to have happened for Stan to be calling her.

Suddenly chilled, she was scared something had happened to Nick or one of their other brothers.

"Talia, it's Stan," he said when she answered. "Can I come see you? I'm in Dallas."

"Of course. I'm in a condo. Let me give you the address. Is everything all right?"

"Oh, yeah. I have a present for Hattie."

She let out the breath she'd been holding and smiled. She missed Stan. Just as she missed Nick and all of them. "Sure. I'll be so glad to see you. Come on." She gave him her address and went to get Hattie ready for company.

She changed out of the yoga pants she wore to unpack boxes, dressing in red slacks, a red cotton blouse and red high-heeled sandals. She ran a brush through her curls and then turned to pick up Hattie and get her changed into a yellow playsuit. "Your uncle Stan is coming to see you. He has a surprise for you."

"Prize?"

"Oh, yes. Your uncles shower you with presents almost as much as your daddy did."

"Da," Hattie repeated as Talia's phone chimed again. But this time she saw Nick was calling. And this time she answered.

"Hi. I'm in Dallas and would like to come talk to you."

She closed her eyes, hurting, remembering the words that had passed between them and thinking about her pregnancy. She hadn't figured out yet when and how she would tell him. She remembered clearly that he'd said he didn't want any more children.

"Talia? Are you there? I really want to see you. Where are you?"

"Stan is on his way over. He'll be here any minute. Does he know you're coming?"

"No, he doesn't. Give me your address."

She did and he told her he would see her soon.

She stared into space. She couldn't tell him yet about the pregnancy. Not with Stan here.

It was another twenty minutes before her doorbell chimed, and she went to the door to open it and face Stan. He hugged her lightly and kissed her cheek. Hattie stood with her hand in Talia's and Stan knelt to pick her up.

"How's my pretty Hattie?"

She poked his chest with her finger and wrapped her arms around his neck.

"Hey, she remembers me."

Talia smiled. "Of course she does."

"Hattie, I brought you a present," he said, giving the little girl a pink sack with a pink silk bow with bells on it. She shook the sack, making the bells jingle, and she laughed. "Hattie, you have a present in the sack," Stan said.

"I think you've brought her a very fascinating sack. It'll take a while to get to the present." She led him into the living room, where they sat down. "Stan, Nick called after you did. He's on his way here. Did you know he was coming?"

"No. He didn't know he was coming earlier when I talked to him. Talia, I know he's hurt, but we had words. I told him I was going to come here and ask you to get a divorce and then propose to you. I'm sure my brothers will feel the same way." Before she could say anything, Stan continued. "Nick is just hurt and not thinking. I guess I shook him up if he's on his way to see you, so I'll get out of here. Just don't get out of the family too fast. We all want you back at the ranch and we miss Hattie."

She laughed and kissed his cheek. "You're great, Stan. I'm not leaving the family yet, but I don't know about Nick."

"Well, if you're not married to him, you can take your choice of me or Blake or Adam. But I'm the most fun," he said and she laughed again.

"That's an almost irresistible proposal, Stan. Thank you."

He stood up and handed Hattie to her. "I'm going to run. Show Hattie her present when she's through playing with the sack. I don't want to cross paths with Nick right now."

"Ahh, she has her new toy," Talia said, watching Hattie pull a furry toy kitten out of the sack and hug it. The child let out a squeal of delight.

"It's a windup toy, Hattie," Stan explained, reaching out to show her. But Hattie merely clutched it to her chest. "Looks like she'd rather hug it."

He went to the door to see himself out. "Good luck dealing with my brother, Talia. Remember, three more Duncans love you."

She smiled at him. "Thanks, Stan. That's sweet."

He smiled. "'Bye, Hattie. I love you."

He hadn't been gone twenty minutes when the doorbell rang, and she opened the door to face Nick.

Nine

"Come in," she said, hating that she was breathless. He looked more handsome than ever in jeans, a long-sleeved tan Western shirt and his black boots. More than anything she just wanted to walk into his arms, but she wasn't going back to the life they'd had when she left him. Why was he here?

He came in, and Hattie hurried to him, holding out her thin arms. "Da."

"Hattie," he said, picking her up to hug her. "I love you," he said, closing his eyes, and Talia hurt for him even though she was upset with him. How could he not pour out his love to his baby girl?

Talia felt a dull ache. She wanted Nick's arms around her. She wanted him to hold her, to kiss her.

She looked at his hands as he held Hattie. She could remember his hands too well, his fingers so light, so sexy, moving over her, caressing her.

"Talia." His voice penetrated her errant thoughts and she met his eyes.

He stood there holding Hattie, staring at her. He moved a step closer, holding Hattie with one arm, placing his other hand on her shoulder. "I want you and Hattie in my life. I love you, Talia, and I love Hattie."

She could hardly believe her ears. He was uttering the words she had dreamed of, longed to hear, fantasized about. Yet now she couldn't believe them.

"Nick, don't declare love until you're really certain. The last time we were together, you definitely were not in love. If you were, you didn't want to be and you didn't want to acknowledge it." She tried not to think about those nights when they had been together and she'd been in his arms in his bed with his body over hers, with him inside her, his hands taking her out of this world into bliss.

"I think Stan pushed you into this." She steeled herself and held her ground, ignoring the pull of his sexual magnetism. "I have two good teaching offers in colleges. I have a convenient place to live. I'm set here in Dallas and I think we need to step back and give each other some room. If next summer you still want us, we'll consider it."

"I didn't come because of Stan. I came because I've missed you and I've been miserable without you. You were right, Talia. You just have to live with risks. That's part of life. Loss is part of life, but hopefully, losses are balanced by gains. I need your love and Hattie's. I love you both. Your love and her love make up for the hurt from losses in my life."

"Da?" Hattie said and Nick smiled at her as she ran her fingers over his chin.

"I'm 'Da' to her."

Then he looked up at Talia and she could swear his eyes were glistening. "When she calls me 'Da,' I don't want to go home without both of you. I've missed you, Talia, and I've missed her more than I would have thought possible. I shouldn't have ever let either of you go."

Her heart drummed. She wanted to believe him, but she had to be sure before she went back and took Hattie, not only for Hattie, but for the child of Nick's she was carrying.

"We need to talk, Nick." Her voice echoed the seriousness she felt. "But we can't talk freely about anything important with Hattie here. Why don't you come in and play with her for a while. She'll take a nap soon and then we can talk."

She led Nick into the small living room of the condo.

"Can I take the two of you out to dinner?" he asked her as he followed.

She turned to him and shook her head. "Thank you, Nick, but no. I'm still getting settled here and I've got things to move around and unpack."

"I can send some guys from the ranch to help you, but I'd prefer you come home."

Talia didn't react to his offer. Either of them. Instead, she handed him one of Hattie's favorite toys. Hearing her unspoken answer, Nick sat on the floor and began to play with Hattie.

"I'll go get us cold drinks," she said. "What would you like?"

"A cold beer? Do you have any?"

"Sorry, I don't."

"I'll drink water."

It was an hour later, deep into the afternoon, before Hattie fell asleep. The whole time Talia sat there, watching Nick and his daughter, she felt her resolve weakening. Seeing him with Hattie was melting her. He was enraptured by the baby's every move, every sound, as she played with her doll and her bunny. Talia didn't want to admit it, but how could she fool herself? She was still in love with her husband.

By the time Nick carried Hattie to her crib and came back into the living room, Talia was like a firecracker with a short fuse. He went to her and reached down to take her hand and pull her to her feet. His arms went around her, and when she looked into his eyes, her heart thudded against her ribs.

Desire flashed in her, hot, insistent. She wanted his kisses, his hands on her, his body against hers. The last of her reserve and coolness vanished. One look from his green eyes and she was sizzling with longing, wanting him desperately.

"Talia, I've missed you. Come home," he whispered into her ear. "I want you."

And she wanted him. Right now every nerve ending in her body cried out for him. But it wasn't about what she wanted anymore. It was about what Hattie needed.

She stepped back so that she could look into his eyes. "What about Hattie? Are you really ready to give her your love, attention and time? To come in before she falls asleep at night? You have enough money that you could sit on your porch and rock for the rest of your life and never have to work, so when you work until nine or ten and your baby is sound asleep and you leave before sunup, you send the message that she isn't important to you. That you don't love her. I didn't expect love for me, but I did for your child."

"I am so sorry, Talia. I do love her and I miss her and every day is important with her because she grows so fast. I love her and I'll show her every day. I'll leave after her breakfast and come home for supper with her. How's that?

"You really mean all that you're saying?" Talia asked, her heart beating faster.

"Yes, I do. I promise. I love Hattie and I'll spend my days proving it to you. And to her."

She stared at him, trying to decide if he would keep his promise.

"And I love you, Talia," he said softly, cupping her cheeks in his palms.

She gazed into his green-gold eyes and her heart beat faster. But she had to know...

"Nick, don't tell me that unless you're sure," she said.

"I'm very sure," he replied. "I almost lost you because of feeling sorry for myself and thinking too much about myself. But I've changed, Talia. I love you and I miss you. If you come home, I'll show you how much."

He stole her breath with a kiss. A passionate, possessive kiss that made her weak in the knees and intensified the ache for him low inside her. She wanted his hands and his mouth all over her.

He wanted her, too; she could feel his hardness pressed against her thigh. But would that change when he learned her news? Would he still want her to go home with him?

Struggling with her thoughts and fears, she pushed him away. Her breath was ragged when she spoke. "Nick, I need to tell you something. Please sit."

He picked her up and sat in a chair with her on his lap.

She shook her head. "This isn't what I had in mind, because I don't think you're going to be happy. In a few minutes, I think you'll want to say goodbye and go home alone." Her heart ached as she said the words.

He shook his head and framed her face with his

hands. "There's nothing you can tell me that can change the way I feel. I love you and I want you in my life always."

"I'll give you a chance to say that again and this first time won't count. Right after I give you my news." She drew a deep breath and blurted it out.

"Nick, I'm pregnant with your baby."

He stared at her as if he couldn't understand what she'd said.

"I'm carrying your baby now," she repeated. "I know that's not what you wanted. You told me you had enough and you didn't want any more children. Now, I've had two miscarriages, so I don't know what will happen with this third pregnancy. They couldn't find why I miscarried those first two times, but the doctor says so far everything looks fine this time. The baby's due next spring and—"

She realized she was babbling and she stopped herself. She looked deep in Nick's eyes and tried to read his thoughts. But failed. When he finally opened his mouth to speak, she steeled herself for his response, knowing he would rescind his offer, his declarations of forever love.

"I want you to come home with me and let me take care of you and our baby. That's really what I want with all my heart."

She stared at him, not believing her own ears. He wanted the baby? He wanted her?

"Nick, don't tell me that if you don't mean it."

"I mean it." A smile broke out across his lips and

he hugged her. "We're going to have a baby. Oh, Talia. I want you to come home with me. I want this baby."

"That's a complete turnaround from what you told me before."

"Yes, it is, but I've been around Hattie more and I've done without both of you in my life and that was worst of all. I'm willing to take those risks. I love you."

Her heart thundered so hard she thought it'd burst with joy. But before she could show him how happy she was, he stood up and put her carefully in the chair.

"I have to go out to my truck. I'll be back in a minute."

She went to the window, and she saw him in his truck looking down at something he must have in his hands. When he came back inside, she stood there waiting for him. "What are you doing?"

He crossed the room to her. "Talia Duncan, I love you with all my heart. And I love little Hattie. I want both of you to come back home so I can take care of you. And I want our baby. *Our baby*—that sounds wonderful. You'll carry this baby and Hattie will have a little brother or a little sister."

Tears stung her eyes and she slipped her arms around his neck. "Nick, you better mean what you say," she whispered before she kissed him.

His arm banded her waist tightly and he held her

pressed against him. "Call your doctor tomorrow and see if we can have sex while you're pregnant."

She laughed. "That wasn't what caused my miscarriages and I can answer that. Yes, we can. This is very early in this pregnancy."

"I brought Hattie a present." He held up a small gift bag. "I got you one, too."

"Nick," she said, smiling. "Stop buying so much for Hattie. She'll be spoiled rotten."

"No, she won't. Impossible. She's way too sweet. Here's your present, Talia." He reached into the bag and pulled out a small box wrapped in white paper and tied with a big blue silk bow.

"Oh, Nick." From the size of the box, she guessed it was a bracelet to match the pendant he had given her. She tore the wrappings away and opened the box to see another fancy box, a much smaller one, that she opened. A dazzling diamond ring was nestled against black velvet.

"Nick, this is gorgeous."

He took it out of the box. "We married for convenience and I only gave you a wedding band. Now this is for love and this ring I got for you out of love. I want the world to know I love you and you're my bride." He took her hand and slipped the ring on her finger.

"Oh, Nick, I love it!" she said as she threw her arms around his neck and kissed him. His arms banded her waist again and he leaned over her to kiss her long and passionately, making her heart race and filling her with joy.

"Hey," he said, leaning back and looking down at her. "You're crying."

"They're tears of joy. I never thought I'd hear you say you loved me, but you did. I love you with all my heart and I know we're going to have a wonderful family. Nick, you will always miss Regina and Artie and your mom and your grandmother, but you're going to be showered with love by me, by Hattie and by our little baby."

He lowered his hand to her still-flat belly, as if to embrace their unborn baby. "I almost made the biggest mistake of my life, but I was already on my way to fixing it because I had that ring made for you two weeks ago."

She gazed into his green eyes and her heart pounded with joy. "Nick, I just know I won't miscarry this time. We'll have our babies, and Hattie will have a little brother or sister. You really did give me the world when you married me—your love, Hattie as my daughter, a new baby, your family's love. You have the money, sweetie, but I have the riches." She cradled his jaw and rained kisses over his face. "As long as we have each other's love and our little babies, we'll have everything. Everything worth risking your heart for." She set one last kiss on his lips. "I love you."

"And I love you, darlin', with all my being. Now I

can tell those brothers of mine that not one of them is going to get you to leave me and marry him."

She laughed as she hugged him and leaned close again to kiss him. "I'm all yours. I love you, my handsome Texas rancher."

* * * * *

Notorious playboy Nolan Madaris is determined to escape his great-grandmother's famous matchmaking schemes, but Ivy Chapman, the woman his great-grandmother has picked out for him, is nothing like he expects—and she's got her own proposal for how to get their meddling families off their backs and out of their love lives!

*Read on for a sneak peek of
BEST LAID PLANS,
the latest in* New York Times *bestselling author
Brenda Jackson's
MADARIS FAMILY SAGA!*

Prologue

Christmas Day

Nolan Madaris III took a sip of his beer while standing on the balcony of his condo. Leaning against the rail, he had a breathtaking view of the exclusive fifteen-story Madaris Building that was surrounded by a cluster of upscale shops, restaurants and a beautiful jogging park with a huge man-made pond. The condos where he lived were right across from the water.

The entire complex, including the condos, had been architecturally designed, engineered and constructed by the Madaris Construction Company that was owned by his cousins Blade and Slade. For the holidays, the Madaris Building and the surrounding shops, restaurants and jogging park were beautifully decorated with colorful, bright lights. It was hard to believe a new year was just a week away.

When Nolan had arrived home from his cousin Lee's wedding, he hadn't bothered to remove his tuxedo. Instead he'd headed straight for the refrigerator, grabbed a beer and proceeded to the balcony for a bit of mental relaxation. But all his mind could do was recall the moment his ninetysomething-year-old great-grandmother, Felicia Laverne Madaris, had finally cornered him at the reception that evening. She was a notorious matchmaker, and he'd been avoiding her all night. Her success rate was too astounding to suit him—and she had calmly warned him that he was next.

He was just as determined not to be.

Nolan, his brother, Corbin, and his cousins Reese and Lee had all been born within a fifteen-month period. They were as close as brothers and had been thick as thieves while growing up. Mama Laverne swore her goal was to marry them all off before she took her last breath. They all told her that wouldn't happen, but then the next thing they knew, Reese had married Kenna and today Lee married Carly.

What bothered Nolan more than anything about his great-grandmother setting her schemes on him was that she of all people knew what he'd gone through with Andrea Dunmire. Specifically, the hurt, pain and humiliation she had caused him. Yes, it had been years ago and he had gotten over it, but there were some things you didn't forget. A woman ripping your heart out of your chest was one of them.

His cell phone rang. Recognizing the ringtone, he pulled it out of his pocket and answered, "Yes, Corbin?"

"Hey, man, I just wanted to check on you. We saw you tear out of here like the devil himself was after you. It's Christmas and we thought you would stay the night at Whispering Pines and continue to party like the rest of us."

Whispering Pines was their uncle Jake's ranch. Nolan took another sip of his beer before saying, "I couldn't stay knowing Mama Laverne is already plotting my downfall. You wouldn't believe what she told me."

"We weren't standing far away and heard."

Nolan shook his head in frustration. "So now all of you know that Mama Laverne's friend's grand-daughter is the woman she's picked out for me."

"Yes, and we got a name. Reese and I overheard Mama Laverne tell Aunt Marilyn that your future wife's name is Ivy Chapman."

"Like hell the woman is my future wife." And Nolan couldn't care less about her name. He'd never met her and didn't intend to. "All this time I thought Mama Laverne was plotting to marry the woman's granddaughter off to Lee. She set me up real good."

Corbin didn't say anything and Nolan was glad because for the moment he needed the silence. It didn't matter to him one iota that so far every one of his cousins whose wives had been selected by his great-grandmother were madly in love with their spouses and saw her actions as a blessing and not a curse. What mattered was that she should not have interfered in the process. And what bothered him more than anything was knowing that he was next on her list. He didn't want her to find him a wife. When and if he was ready for marriage, he was certainly capable of finding one on his own.

"You've come up with a plan?" Corbin interrupted Nolan's thoughts to ask.

Nolan thought of the diabolical plan his cousin Lee had put in place to counteract their great-grandmother's shenanigans and guaranteed to outsmart Mama Laverne for sure. However, in the end, Lee's plan had backfired.

"No, why waste my time planning anything? I simply refuse to play the games Mama Laverne is intent on playing. What I'm going to do is ignore her foolishness and enjoy my life as the newest eligible Madaris bachelor."

He could say that since, at thirty-four, he was ten months older than Corbin, who would be next on their great-grandmother's hit list. "By the time I make my rounds, there won't be a single woman living in Houston who won't know I'm not marriage material," Nolan added.

Corbin chuckled. "That sounds like a plan to me."

"Not a plan, just stating my intentions. I refuse

to let Mama Laverne shove a wife that I don't want down my throat just because she thinks she can and that she should."

After ending the call with his brother, Nolan swallowed the last of his beer. Like he'd told Corbin, he didn't have a plan and wouldn't waste time coming up with one. What he intended to do was to have fun; as much fun as any single man could possibly have.

A huge smile touched his lips as he left the balcony. Walking into his condo, he headed for his bedroom. Quickly removing the tux, he changed into a pair of slacks and a pullover sweater. The night was still young and there was no reason for him not to go out and celebrate the holiday.

As he moved toward his front door, he started humming "Jingle Bells." *Let the fun begin.*

One

Fifteen months later...

Nolan clicked off his mobile phone, satisfied with the call he'd just ended with Lee about his cousin's newest hotel, the Grand MD Paris. Construction of the huge mega-structure had begun three weeks ago. Already it was being touted by the media as the hotel of the future, and Nolan would have to agree.

Due to the hotel's intricate design and elaborate formation, the estimated completion time was two years. You couldn't rush grandeur, and by the time the doors opened, the Grand MD Paris would set itself apart as one of the most luxurious hotels in the world.

This would be the third hotel Lee and his business partner, DeAngelo Di Meglio, had built. First there had been the Grand MD Dubai, and after such astounding success with that hotel, the pair had opened the Grand MD Vegas. Since both hotels had been doing extremely well financially, a decision was made to build a third hotel in Paris. The Grand MD Paris would use state-of-the-art technology while maintaining the rich architectural designs Paris was known for.

Slade, the architect in the Madaris family, had designed all three Grand MD hotels. Nolan would have to say that Slade's design of the Paris hotel was nothing short of a masterpiece. Slade had made sure that no Grand MD hotel looked the same and that each had its own unique architecture and appeal. Slade's twin, Blade, was the structural engineer and had spent the last six months in Paris making sure the groundwork was laid before work on the hotel began. There had been surveys that needed to be completed, soil samples to analyze, as well as a tight construction schedule if they were to meet the deadline for a grand opening two years from now. And knowing Lee and DeAngelo like he did, Nolan expected the Grand MD Paris to open its doors on time and to a fanfare of the likes of a presidential inauguration.

After getting a master's graduate degree at MIT, Nolan had begun working for Chenault Electronics at their Chicago office. Chenault Electronics was considered one of the top ten electronics companies in the world. The owner, Nicholas Chenault, was a family friend, had taken Nolan under his wing and had not only been his boss but his mentor, as well.

After working for Chenault for eight years, Nolan had returned to Houston three years ago to start his own company, Madaris Innovations.

Nolan's company would provide all the electronic and technology work for the Grand MD Paris; some would be the first of its kind anywhere. All high-tech and trend changing. It would be Nolan's first project of this caliber and he appreciated Lee and DeAngelo for giving him the opportunity. Lee and his wife, Carly, spent most of their time in Paris now. Since DeAngelo and his wife, Peyton, were expecting their first child four months from now, DeAngelo had decreased his travel schedule somewhat.

Nolan also appreciated Nicholas for agreeing to partner with him on the project. Chenault Electronics would be bringing years of experience and know-how to the table and Nolan welcomed Nicholas's skill and knowledge.

Nolan had enjoyed the two weeks he'd spent in Paris. He would have to go back a number of times this year for more meetings and he looked forward to doing so, since Paris was one of his favorite places to visit. There was a real possibility that he might have to live there while his electronic equipment was scheduled to be installed.

Nolan leaned back in his chair. In a way, he regretted returning to Houston. Before leaving, he had done everything in his power to become the life of every party, and his reputation as Houston's number one playboy had been cemented. In some circles, he'd been pegged as Houston's One-Night Stander. Now that he was back, that role had to be rekindled, but if he was honest with himself, he wasn't looking forward to the nights of mindless, emotionless sex with women whose names he barely remembered. He only hoped that Ivy Chapman, her grandmother and his great-grandmother were getting the message—he had no intentions of settling down anytime soon. At least not in the next twenty-five years or so.

He rubbed a hand down his face, thinking that while he wouldn't admit to it, he was discovering that living the life of a playboy wasn't all that it was cracked up to be. Most of his dates were one-night stands. There were times he would spend a week with the same woman, and occasionally someone would make it a month, but he didn't want to give these women the wrong idea about the possibility of a future together. He was probably going to have to change his phone number due to the number of messages from women wanting a callback. Women expecting a callback. Women he barely remembered from one sexual encounter to the next. Jeez.

Nolan wondered how his cousins Clayton and Blade, the ones who'd been known as die-hard womanizers in the family before they'd settled down to marry, had managed it all. Clayton had had such an active sex life that he'd owned a case of condoms that he'd kept in his closet. Nolan knew that tidbit was more fact than fiction, since he'd seen the case after Clayton had passed it on to Blade when Clayton had gotten married.

Blade hadn't passed the box on to anyone when he'd married. Not only had he used up the case he'd gotten from Clayton, but he'd gone through a case of his own. Somehow Clayton and Blade had not only managed to handle the playboy life, but each claimed they'd enjoyed doing so immensely at the time.

Nolan, on the other hand, was finding the life of a Casanova pretty damn taxing and way too demanding. And it wasn't even deterring Ivy Chapman.

Nolan picked up the envelope on top of the stack on his desk. He knew what it was and who it had come from. He recalled getting the first one six months ago and he had received several more since then. He wondered why Ivy Chapman was still sending him these little personal notes when he refused to acknowledge them. All the notes said the same thing... *Nolan, I would love to meet you. Call me so it can be arranged. Here is my number...*

Nolan didn't give a royal flip what her phone number was, since he had no intentions of calling her, regardless of the fact that his matchmaking great-grandmother fully expected him to do so. He would continue to ignore Miss Chapman and any correspondence she sent him. He refused to give in to his great-grandmother's matchmaking shenanigans.

He tossed the envelope aside and picked up his

cell phone to call his family and let them know he was back. He had slept off jet lag most of yesterday and hadn't talked to anyone other than his cousin Reese and his brother, Corbin. Reese and his wife, Kenna, were expecting their first baby in June and everyone was excited. For years, Reese and Kenna, who'd met in college, had claimed they were nothing but best friends. However, the family had known better and figured one day the couple would reach the same conclusion. Mama Laverne bragged that they were just another one of her success stories.

Nolan ended the call with his parents, stood and walked over to the window to look out. Like most of his relatives, he leased space in the Madaris Building. His electronics company was across the hall from Madaris Explorations, owned by his older cousin Dex.

He loved Houston in March, but it always brought out dicey weather. You had some warm days, but there were days when winter refused to fade into the background while spring tried emerging. He was ready for warmer days and couldn't wait to spend time at the cottage he'd purchased on Tiki Island, a village in Galveston, last year. He'd hired Ron Siskin, a property manager, to handle the leasing of the cottage whenever he wasn't using it. So far it had turned out to be not only a great investment but also a getaway place whenever he needed a break from the demands of his job, life itself and, yes, of course, the women who were becoming more demanding by the hour.

The buzzer sounded and he walked back over to his desk. "Yes, Marlene?" Marlene was an older woman in her sixties who'd worked for him since he started the company three years ago. A retired administrative assistant for an insurance agent, Marlene had decided to come out of retirement when she'd gotten bored. She was good at what she did and helped to keep the office running when he was in or out of it.

"There's a woman here to see you, Mr. Madaris. She doesn't have an appointment and says it's important."

Nolan frowned, glancing at his watch. It's wasn't even ten in the morning. Who would show up at his office without an appointment and at this hour? There were a number of family members who worked in the Madaris Building. Obviously, it wasn't one of them; otherwise Marlene would have said so. "Who is she?"

"A Miss Ivy Chapman."

He guessed she was tired of sending notes that went unanswered. Hadn't she heard around town what a scoundrel he was? The last man any woman should be interested in? So what was she doing here?

There was only one way to find out. If she needed to know why he hadn't responded, that he could certainly tell her. She could stop sending him those notes or else he would take her actions as a form of harassment. He had no problem telling her in no un-certain terms that he was not interested in pursuing an affair with her, regardless of the fact that his great-grandmother and her grandmother wanted it to be so.

"Send her in, Marlene."

"Yes, Mr. Madaris."

Nolan had eased into his jacket and straightened his tie before his office door swung open. The first thing he saw was a huge bouquet of flowers that was bigger than the person carrying them. Why was the woman bringing him flowers? Did she honestly think a huge bouquet of flowers would work when her cute little notes hadn't?

He couldn't see the woman's face behind the huge vase of flowers, and without saying a word, not even so much as a good morning, she plopped the monstrosity onto his desk with a loud thump. It was a wonder the vase hadn't cracked. Hell, maybe it had. He could just imagine water spilling all over his desk.

Nolan looked from the flowers that were taking up entirely too much space on his desk to the woman who'd unceremoniously placed them there. He was not prepared for the beauty of the soft brown eyes behind a pair of thick-rimmed glasses or the perfect roundness of her face and the creamy cocoa coloring of her complexion. And he couldn't miss the fullness of her lips that were pursed tight in anger.

"I'm only going to warn you but this once, Nolan Madaris. Do not send me any more flowers. Doing so won't change a thing. I've decided to come tell you personally, the same thing I've repeatedly told your great-grandmother and my grandmother. There is no way I'd ever become involved with you. No way. Ever."

Her words shocked him to the point that he could only stand there and stare at her. She crossed her arms over her chest and stared back. "Well?" she asked in a voice filled with annoyance when he continued to stare at her and say nothing. "Do I make myself clear?"

Finding his voice, Nolan said, "You most certainly do. However, there's a problem and I consider it a major one."

Those beautiful eyes were razor-sharp and directed at him. "And just what problem is that?"

Now it was he who turned a cutting gaze on her. "I never sent you any flowers. Today or ever."

Find out if Nolan Madaris has finally
met his match in
BEST LAID PLANS
by New York Times *bestselling author*
Brenda Jackson, available March 2018
wherever HQN Books and ebooks are sold.

www.Harlequin.com

#2581 CLAIM ME, COWBOY
Copper Ridge • by Maisey Yates
Wanted: fake fiancée for a wealthy rancher to teach his father not to play matchmaker. Benefits: your own suite in a rustic mansion and money to secure your baby's future. Rules: deny all sizzling sexual attraction and don't fall in love!

#2582 EXPECTING A SCANDAL
Texas Cattleman's Club: The Impostor • by Joanne Rock
Wealthy trauma surgeon Vaughn Chambers spends his days saving lives and his nights riding the ranch. But when it comes to healing his own heart, he finds solace only in the arms of Abigail Stewart, who's pregnant with another man's baby...

#2583 UPSTAIRS DOWNSTAIRS BABY
Billionaires and Babies • by Cat Schield
Single mom Claire Robbins knows her boss is expected to marry well. Taking up with the housekeeper is just not done—especially if her past catches up to her. Falling for Linc would be the ultimate scandal. But she's never been good at resisting temptation...

#2584 THE LOVE CHILD
Alaskan Oil Barons • by Catherine Mann
When reclusive billionaire rancher Trystan Mikkelson is thrust into the limelight, he needs a media makeover! Image consultant Isabeau Waters guarantees she can turn him into the face of his family's empire. But one night of passion leads to pregnancy, and it could cost them everything.

#2585 THE TEXAN'S WEDDING ESCAPE
Heart of Stone • by Charlene Sands
Rancher Cooper Stone owes the Abbott family a huge debt...and he's been tasked with stopping Lauren Abbott from marrying the wrong man! But how can Lauren trust her feelings when she learns her time with Cooper is a setup?

#2586 HIS BEST FRIEND'S SISTER
First Family of Rodeo • by Sarah M. Anderson
Family scandal chases expectant mother Renee from New York City to Texas. But when rodeo and oil tycoon Oliver, her brother's best friend, agrees to hide her in his Dallas penthouse, sparks fly. Will her scandal ruin him, too?

Get 2 Free Books,
Plus 2 Free Gifts—
just for trying the Reader Service!

Joshua Grayson looked out the window of his office and did
not feel the kind of calm he ought to feel.

He'd moved back to Copper Ridge six months ago from
Seattle, happily trading in a man-made, rectangular skyline
for the natural curve of the mountains.

But right now he doubted anything would decrease the
tension he was feeling from dealing with the fallout of his
father's ridiculous ad. Another attempt by the old man to
make Joshua live the life his father wanted him to.

The only kind of life his father considered successful: a
wife, children.

He couldn't understand why Joshua didn't want the same.

No. That kind of life was for another man, one with
another past and another future. It was not for Joshua. And
that was why he was going to teach his father a lesson.

He wasn't responsible for the ad in a national paper
asking for a wife, till death do them part. But an unsuitable,
temporary wife? Yes. That had been his ad.

He was going to win the game. Once and for all. And the woman he hoped would be his trump card was on her way.

The doorbell rang and he stood up behind his desk. She was here. And she was—he checked his watch—late.

A half smile curved his lips.

Perfect.

He took the stairs two at a time. He was impatient to meet his temporary bride. Impatient to get this plan started so it could end.

He strode across the entryway and jerked the door open. And froze.

The woman standing on his porch was small. And young, just as he'd expected, but… She wore no makeup, which made her look like a damned teenager. Her features were fine and pointed; her dark brown hair hung lank beneath a ragged beanie that looked like it was in the process of unraveling while it sat on her head.

He didn't bother to linger over the rest of the details—her threadbare sweater with too-long sleeves, her tragic skinny jeans—because he was stopped, immobilized really, by the tiny bundle in her arms.

A baby.

His prospective bride had come with a baby.

Well, hell.

Don't miss
CLAIM ME, COWBOY
by New York Times *bestselling author Maisey Yates,*
part of her **COPPER RIDGE** *series!*

Available April 2018 wherever
Harlequin® Desire books and ebooks are sold.

www.Harlequin.com

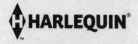

LOVE
Harlequin
romance?

Join our Harlequin community to share your thoughts and connect with other romance readers!

Be the first to find out about promotions, news, and exclusive content!

Sign up for the Harlequin e-newsletter and download a free book from any series at **www.TryHarlequin.com**

CONNECT WITH US AT:

Harlequin.com/Community

 Facebook.com/HarlequinBooks

 Twitter.com/HarlequinBooks

 Instagram.com/HarlequinBooks

 Pinterest.com/HarlequinBooks

ReaderService.com

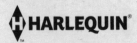 **HARLEQUIN**®

**ROMANCE WHEN
YOU NEED IT**

HSOCIAL2017

Reward the book lover in you!

Earn points from all your Harlequin book purchases from wherever you shop.

Turn your points into *FREE BOOKS* of your choice
OR
EXCLUSIVE GIFTS from your favorite authors or series.

Join for FREE today at
www.HarlequinMyRewards.com.

Harlequin My Rewards is a free program (no fees) without any commitments or obligations.

MYR17